1/24/12

Mike!

It has been my great pleasure working side by side with you. Caw! Caw! You bring a smile to my face on days when nothing else can. Keep learning those funny dances you do to cheer us up. May you always follow your dreams! ♡,

yu Murray

St. Louis Publishers Association Contest Finalist
Medallion used with permission.
www.stlouispublishers.org

Book interior design by Annie Yi-Chieh Liao
www.annieliao.com

Cover Photography © Yolanda Ciolli
Models: Megan Meier, Jeff Schlotzhauer, Nicole Niziolek

Cover design by Yolanda Ciolli
www.yolandaciolli.com

Cover Art Paper by Leandra Spangler
www.bearcreekpaperworks.com

Editing by Katherine Pickett, P.O.P. Editorial Services
www.popediting.net

Published by AKA-Publishing
Columbia, Missouri
www.aka-publishing.com

ISBN: 978-1-936688-03-6

AKA-Publishing.com

OIL IN THE WOK

YuMin Ye

To Mom & Dad, friends, family,
and Woodcrest Home Group

OIL IN THE WOK

I was trying to imagine "Amber Yang" in neon pink and green flashing marquee lights, then thought yellow lights might have been more fitting.

Nah. That couldn't happen. I was and always would be Amber Yang. Never *the* Amber Yang. Never the most talked about Yang in the whole history of China, which included ancient China, of course. Just plain old Amber, only daughter of Mark and Iris, completely unrelated to the singer.

I'd been having trouble sleeping. Must have been insomnia or something—maybe those growing pains I read about somewhere. That was it. Maybe it was like one of those midlife crises that older people went through, except for teenagers. Or maybe I just aged fast.

For the past nine years I'd been trying, subconsciously of course, to figure out who I was. Mom once told me that I knew how to sing before I knew how to talk and that I was better at it, too. She sent me to ballet lessons at the age of three, but finding myself no good at it, I quit four years later. That was when I began to draw. I suspect I inherited the artsy gene from Dad. A fashion designer, he was recently cut from *Holly Doll*, a sitcom for young girls who love clothes and love playing dress-up. Working on clothing designs for the show kept him busy, and he had a way of missing out. His career had just come to a screeching halt. They told him his designs weren't chic enough. I had no idea what that meant, as I had never ventured into the fashion world, but I was pretty sure it was a big insult. So he was back to working at Co~Z Monster, the local café, making coffee to help the overweight become morbidly obese. Oh, and getting on Mom's nerves. I bet they couldn't go *one* day without fighting, and now things had been looking sour, especially for Dad. Once, I did an oil painting of them fighting. I took a snapshot when they weren't paying attention, developed the picture, and created a likeness. Ironically, Mom said it was some of my best work. She framed it and hung it on their bedroom wall, above the bedpost. She had all my paintings framed.

Considering that it was my junior year, I probably should have been applying to art school. But I was not. I wanted to start singing again. I didn't know where it would take me, but I had an idea of where I wanted to go. The problem was…no one knew about it yet. It was not exactly a popular choice with my parents. Neither was art school, but the 'rents thought I could do painting until I figured out what I'm really going to do. For as long as I could remember, my parents had wanted me to get into medical school. It was such common knowledge that even Mr. Frasca, my Chemistry teacher from the year before, labeled my condition as "the Chinese way."

When I think of my Chemistry teacher, I

first think of his hair. Mr. Frasca was balding and the few strands left here and there were white. He had two sons, and the eldest was about to turn twenty-eight this year. I don't know how long he had been teaching, but Mr. Frasca looked ancient. At the very least I could surmise that he had enough Chinese students over the years to come up with a name for my condition, as it were. That's cool. It would have been even cooler if I could have gotten him to convince my parents that I wasn't going to follow "the Chinese way." Yeah, maybe on the day the sky's made of blueberry ice cream.

My plan was to cut a demo, send it off to various record companies, get signed, sell billions of LPs, get noticed by the media, and land my first acting gig all by the time I turned twenty. Why twenty? No particular reason. I just happened to like that number. And…it was not that far into the future. Why acting? Well, it just seemed that if you were a singer, then you had to be an actor as well. (In my case, actress.)

There was just one problem with this plan: if I didn't let my parents know what I was up to soon, I might not even get a chance to sing "do-re-mi." But for now, I had to figure out a way to nip this insomnia in the bud or I'd be going crazy soon! Thankfully the next day was Friday, so after I forced my butt to get up, get to school, and make it through all my classes, I could finally drive me and my beat-up old car to my favorite spot by the Hoop, otherwise known as the Hope Court. Maybe I'd even get in some balling time. After all, they say physical activity can cure sleeping problems. Either way, I had to get to the Hoop; it was my secret place where I liked to hang and hide from everyone. And when I say everyone, I *mean* everyone.

My head hurt. For the past minute I had been counting to sixty until the green numbers on my digital alarm clock changed from 5:59 to 6:00. It didn't specify a.m. or p.m., but that's the beauty of looking out the window. People are smart, you know. They used to look at the shadow of a stick to mark the position of the sun and tell what time of day it was. And then suddenly, voilà! The clock is invented.

I wished I could have used some of those sleepless nights and early mornings to do something productive—like cut a demo or something. Or at least research record companies on the Net. It occurred to me that I hadn't the slightest clue as to how to get started.

My brain was about to crack. As much as I wanted to set my devious plan in motion, I had to worry about my AP classes—and that included AP Studio Art, which I signed up for at the last minute, in case I was going to apply to an art school, which didn't look likely anymore on account of "the Chinese way." Besides, this was the first serious art course I'd ever taken, and I think you need more than that to get in to art school. I felt like I should have been taking a music class to satisfy my fine arts credit for graduation, but that never happened and I had never been a brave soul to defy and go against the grain.

It was Friday. That was all I cared about at that moment. I sat quietly in my seat because I didn't know anyone in the class. Well, I knew their names, but I hardly think that counts as *knowing*. Since everyone had to take a half year of health class before graduation, I figured junior year would be the perfect time to knock it off my graduation requirement list. It really didn't matter when you took it, just as long as you took it.

I didn't talk to anyone, really. Not just because it was too early in the morning to be making small talk, but also because I had never been good at making new friends. Actually I kind of sucked at it. When I was little I was better at talking to rabbits. I think they were called cottontails. That name's very fitting anyway, if you've ever looked at the tail of one of those brown rabbits—round and white, just like a cotton ball. I would go into the backyard to try to get near one. I'd sit on the roots of our willow tree, watching as they grazed. At the beginning they were afraid of me, never venturing close to the tree, but then they grew bold. I think they were as curious to meet me as I was to watch them eat. I was fascinated with watching them chew, lift their heads up, chew in the air for a bit, then bend down to chew some more. It seemed to me that they only came out when they were hungry, and this repetitive motion was all it took to get full. I envied them in their simplicity.

This was health class and we were working on a group assignment on legalizing marijuana. (Weed, pot, yeah…all that good stuff.) It was one of those dittos that has a statement across the top and a T-chart kind of thing going on, and you have to make a "pro vs. con" list to decide if the statement should become law. Automatically I thought it was kind of juvenile. I mean, the last time I'd seen a ditto like this was maybe third grade. But this was health class and as much as I hated group work—it usually meant I was stuck with the heaviest workload—if I ever wanted to graduate, I had to do this ditto.

When we broke into groups and sat down at our new tables, I found myself sitting right across from one of the few senior guys taking the class. I had never spoken to him before, but from the roll call every morning, I did know his name to be Isaac. He was one of those quiet types, but whenever he had something to say, he was opinionated. I felt lucky to have him in my group. I was quiet too, but unlike him, I did not have a strong opinion about *anything* unless you could count that I hated the taste of mushrooms. Isaac would know how to voice our argument to the class in case we had to present our ideas.

Isaac nodded his head when he saw me. He looked to be a pretty chills person, so I didn't want to act too nervous or too eager to work on the ditto with him. I didn't know what he thought of me, but it probably didn't matter.

"I think marijuana should be legalized," he said solemnly. He averted his eyes as he spoke. He paused.

It seemed that he had been waiting for someone's, *anyone's*, reaction to see how to proceed.

He looked up at no one in particular and when he saw that I was staring at him, he shrugged.

I nodded. I was staring blankly ahead, paying no attention to what was going on around me. Like I said, it was way too early in the morning.

Soon enough, our group fell into silence

while all the other tables were chit-chatting or talking about advantages and disadvantages of their choice already. That's when you know you are stuck in the wrong group! So far, Isaac had stated his opinion. Everyone else had either pretended not to hear or mumbled a nonchalant "yeah." And I...I was mute, as usual, afraid to voice my opinion because I wasn't sure I had an opinion to start with. But it seemed that everyone who took a class with me knew that and wasn't expecting me to contribute much. Well, not orally at least. I tried to act like I didn't care what everyone thought of me, like it didn't matter, but I was only putting up a façade.

I got nervous often, but I never really understood it. It was a mystery to me, like the Loch Ness Monster. Many times I had wished to dive into that lake and find out the secret behind this Monster, but I had failed every single time.

In Spanish class we had learned that the

difference between "soy" and "estoy" was that the former described a characteristic that made you a certain way by character whereas the latter described a state that you were in temporarily and was not permanent. Well, I was "soy nerviosa," not temporarily nervous. I was just a nervous person by nature and it was a part of who I was, something I couldn't easily change. That made me Soy Girl.

Suddenly aware of how quiet our table was, I realized someone had to get the discussion flowing or we were going to be sitting here forever. I even heard Mr. Kurt announce that Group Three (that was our group) wasn't working. So I decided to do something about it. I hated when teachers caught me doing something wrong. I have always hated being criticized by a teacher, ever since I was real little.

"So yeah, you said marijuana should be legalized?" I asked Isaac, so that to Mr. Kurt it looked like we were making some effort now. I felt dumb to be repeating something he said, but it was all I could think of to save our group from the wrath of our health teacher. Then, as soon as I heard what I was saying out loud, I understood what was going on. Wait, make pot legal? As in everyone is *allowed* to get high off of it? That's just not right, I thought. "Why?" I followed up with another question for Isaac, Mr. Opinionated.

He scoffed. "Because everyone's doing weed and getting into a lot of trouble because of it. It's forbidden and that's what makes it so appealing. If we made it legal, then it wouldn't be so thrilling to do it without the fear of getting caught. Eliminate that kind of excitement, then there would be fewer people doing it."

The whole time I was watching him talk passionately about how he felt and it seemed to me that he had already made up his mind about this issue before we even started this assignment. Impressive. I picked up the pen and started writing stuff on the ditto.

"Okay, that makes sense. Should we put legalizing marijuana at the top then?" I felt like an interviewer or a private investigator or one of those detective guys who worked with police officers to solve mysteries at a crime scene. (A crime scene investigator?)

Isaac shrugged. That bothered me. I hated it when people shrugged. For someone so opinionated, it didn't seem like he should be shrugging. I might have been stuck in the gray areas most of the time, but I liked to get direct answers from other people. And then I got it.

"I mean, I really don't see why marijuana shouldn't be legalized," he said.

So I wrote our argument, "Legalize Marijuana," at the top of the T-chart. This was supposed to be a group effort, but it definitely felt like an Isaac and Amber effort instead.

"So…pros and cons…?" I asked, letting

the question hang out in the air, knowing that we were both already getting tired of this assignment. The list on the T-chart below the title was basically full of the reasons Isaac just gave. I could have predicted that and I really wanted to contribute some of my own ideas, but whether it was because I was nervous or had never really thought about the issue before, or a mixture of both, I couldn't come up with anything. Even though Isaac wasn't asking me to come up with pros and cons, when he looked me in the eye, I felt my face go hot. Since he was a chills person, he didn't notice, which made me feel relieved.

When Mr. Kurt asked Group Three to present, Isaac spoke up by default. I think he saw it coming and it didn't bother him at all. I mean, we filled the ditto with *his* ideas. It only made sense that he'd be the one to present them. I sat back and watched as he presented and everyone else in the group got credit along with him. Mr. Kurt nodded his head. We were the last group to present, and Mr. Kurt decided not to collect the dittos. I breathed a sigh of relief as I walked back to my regular seat. The bell was going to ring any minute and for some reason, I felt like for that day I had just finished the hardest class.

Pulling into a parking spot, I shifted the gear to P and turned off the ignition. That Friday afternoon, the Hoop was deserted, except for one little boy, who looked to be about seven or eight years old. Having the court practically to myself was a treat I could not pass up. I had planned on staying no matter what. The Hoop was my sanctuary.

The little boy didn't see me at first. He had on a pair of ripped jeans and a black T-shirt. As I watched him dribble the ball he had in

16

his palms, I couldn't help but wonder which rapper he liked listening to. Was it normal nowadays for kids in elementary school to listen to rap music? Maybe he didn't listen to rap music at all and only liked dressing that way. I didn't know and I didn't want to spend time dwelling on him. But then he noticed me. He said, "Hi, you like to play hoops?"

It always amazed me how brave little kids were. Of course, I couldn't remember ever being that brave when I was that young, but nevertheless, little kids were brave. As usual I stayed quiet and didn't ask him many questions. He told me his name was Jeffrey, and he added that I could call him Jeff. He asked me for my name. I told him Amber. I didn't know how many times I'd actually use the name Jeff, but he was a sweet boy so I couldn't not tell him mine. But that was not all, like almost all little kids, he didn't worry too much about what other people thought about him. Sure, he had normal kid troubles. From what I gathered there was a bully at school who liked to cut in front of him in the lunch line or throw spitballs at him and who knows what else. But he didn't seem to let it bother him too much. He was only seven, yet he already knew that life was unfair. It made me sad, but at the same time, it made my problems seem so small. I mean, the Hoop was not known as the Hope Court for nothing...

When I got home, I found Dad sleeping on the living room couch. He looked like a sack of potatoes. I figured that he'd been up late the night before trying to figure out his next design and had to get up real early to get to Co~Z Monster the following morning. It was obvious that whatever Dad had been working on, he'd been busy. But I knew that it wouldn't matter to Mom. She was going to get into one of her shouting matches with him that night anyway. I knew what they fought about, even though she pretended I knew nothing. Dad had not become the man that Mom wanted to marry. I was prepared for a late-night quarantine in my room.

Mom had tolerated a lot from Dad—his failure to keep a job, his absence from family activities, and even his inability to plan ahead. But now that he got cut again, she had enough. When they met, Dad had aspired to launch his own line some day and Mom had loved him for it. She never thought that twenty years later he'd still be in the same place. Separation was inevitable.

Was it lame that my life had gotten into this monotony? Was it lame that I let my two closest friends make me believe that they really wanted to be friends with me and not because my mom is Dr. Iris Chen, plastic surgeon of every celebrity imaginable? I wanted not to be bitter anymore. I wanted to put it behind me. But the wound was still fresh. Everyone at school thought they knew the real me, but that was only based on what they heard on the street.

Karen. That's one name. Serena. That's another. That's all I had at the moment. But that's all I needed to remember from that night. I had my future to worry about and I also had to reinvent myself. This part was called Reinvention. (This will probably be the only time I ever call it that, but whatever.) Maybe I was meant to be a hermit. Maybe this whole thing with Karen and Serena was a lesson for me. I didn't know much about what was going on with my life, but I did know that I couldn't trust Karen and Serena ever again. No, not after that night. That night was my life's version of Revelation.

I didn't want to think about Revelation. I didn't want to relive every moment in my memory. All I know is, right after it happened, I was left in a state that was less than empty. I can't even tell you what that means. All I can say is, it was a feeling like emptiness and then minus that.

OIL IN THE WOK

Mom had already started the shouting match. When I was little, and the arguments were rare, I used to entertain myself by eavesdropping. Now that the arguing had become as common as breathing, it wasn't so fun anymore.

The time called for an iPod. I used it to drown them out. There was not much going on that night anyway. Naturally I listened to pop. It was not exactly popular at school, as its name implied, but I'd always thought it was the easiest to sing. I loved singing. I'm not your typical sing-in-the-shower type. That's actually not my favorite spot to sing. I prefer singing in places other than the shower, like in my room or in the car. Back when Karen and Serena and I were still friends, we used to sing together and be the all-Chinese Destiny's Child. Those were the good days— before Revelation. With my parents fighting in the background, I just felt like tuning into my iPod and falling asleep. It was still early,

YUMIN YE

but I didn't want to think about anything at that moment. I just wanted to lay back and watch my world disappear temporarily. I liked to fade out and fade in every once in a while.

It was about an hour later and they were still going at it. I checked my phone. No messages. Well, I could have predicted that. It was time to change playlists. I felt like dancing. I didn't really know how, besides my lame ballet moves from way back when, but sometimes there was nothing like a good body dance workout to feel good again, even for a brief moment.

After about twenty minutes of a failed choreography that involved some basic ballet steps and random arm movements, I decided to call it a night. Maybe tomorrow when I wake up, this will all go away or resolve itself, I thought. Then I'll have two days to think or not think until I have to go back to the place we like to call school.

OIL IN THE WOK

As I was preparing to pull into our driveway Monday after school, I was almost happy that the biggest thing on my mind was my AP Bio homework. There's nothing I like more than having to accomplish something so big that it becomes all-consuming and the only thing I worry about for a while. It used to be Karen or Serena who took up all my time, but ever since Revelation, it had been neither. Just then I almost hit the speed limit sign as I noticed a foreign car sitting in our driveway. The license plate read "B F something something."

I threw the car in park and hopped out, leaving the back end askew. I had to get in the house to find out what was going on. I didn't know what to expect. Maybe a huge grasshopper? I stuck the key into the lock and turned, half-expecting to see an enormous blade of grass in our living room, a la <u>James and the Giant Peach</u>.

There was nothing in our living room, no enormous blade of grass or even any unfamiliar jackets for that matter, but I heard voices coming from our guest room down the hall. There were three. One of them was unmistakably my mother's and the other two, I couldn't really tell, but they sounded like my mom's clients. What Dr. Iris Chen's clients were doing in our house, I had no idea, but I figured that they weren't going to stay, whatever they were here for.

I was wrong.

"Amber, is that you?" I could hear Mom calling. I knew I had to answer, but I didn't want to. For the past few weeks, I had been avoiding everyone. I hadn't talked to anyone, not even Celeste, whom I used to go to for everything, in a long time. I was so good at this whole avoiding thing, I bet I could have passed as a recluse. I was not about to meet someone right at that moment, in the middle of my recluse gig.

24

"Yeah," I said. Should I have said "yes" instead? Isn't that the ladylike thing to do: always say "yes" and never "yeah"? Mom had been trying to get me to be more ladylike for a long time, ever since she realized that because I had left China when I was real little I had lost some of that background knowledge on Chinese customs and adopted American ones instead. Well, she tried, but to no avail.

Mom popped her head into the hall and beckoned me to come closer. She looked kind of funny like that, but I did not laugh. In those days it seemed I'd forgotten how to smile. "Come here, I have some people I want you to meet," she said, like she had no idea that I'd been taking refuge in my room ever since Revelation, which I still hadn't really told her about. I suspected that she knew some of it anyway; she just kept her discoveries to herself, as usual. It was part of her DNA as a mother to know intuitively what her daughter was thinking.

25

Brooke Fulton. *The* Brooke Fulton and her mother. They were who my mom called "some people." Brooke wanted to hide out here for a while, in our guest room. A little hiatus from her singing career. Wow. Total pop-star diva at my house! Karen and Serena would just *die* if they found out. Too bad we were not talking anymore, like America and Cuba. Wow. I didn't know how to react, whether I should scream or shout or both. Should I jump up and down and cry, "OH MY GOD!" for a good twenty minutes or so? Pretend to be a crazy, stalking, sycophantic, fawning fan? That sounded about right. But then again, I was not a stalking, crazy fan—at least, not *that* crazy, so I tried to play it cool, even if it was Brooke Fulton.

"This is Brooke Fulton and this is her mom, Lina Fulton," Mom said, as if she were introducing another girl and her mother from school.

At that point I did what anyone would

have done in this situation. I flailed my arms around and tried to utter whatever I could. "You…Brooke…y-you…Brooke Fulton?!" It was real suave, let me tell you.

Both Brooke and her mom laughed, though they were polite about it. Brooke extended her arm to give me her hand and greeted me: "Yes, hi, nice to meet you."

What's my name again? It was so embarrassing that Mom had to tell Brooke herself that my name was Amber. "You better get used to seeing each other around," she commented. "Brooke and Lina are going to be sticking around for a while."

That brought me back to earth again. Wait. My mom, who had been figuring out how to kick Dad out for the past two months, was gonna let a pop star stay here, with us? My mom, of all people, the woman who completely freaked out the one time I asked if Karen could stay with us during spring break while her family jetted off on some adventure somewhere out in the wilderness. She reluctantly agreed, but from then on she told me we were never to have any guests stay over for more than three days ever again. Now she was going to let this burgeoning pop star stay with us indefinitely? There must have been something in our water because the last time I checked, my mom didn't allow her work life to interfere with her personal life. And considering that her family would have fallen under the category of personal, I would have thought having a diva stay with us would have fallen under the category of interfering. Maybe I was overreacting, but that was how I felt.

I wondered what plastic surgery Brooke was considering. Did her mom want plastic surgery, too? Brooke already looked perfect, I thought. What could she possibly want to do to herself? They say that beautiful people have symmetrical faces. Well, I didn't know what kind of face Brooke had, but it was in no way asymmetrical. I supposed that was one of the reasons why she was who she was. She was going to be sharing the guest room with her mom, so I guess that would make her like a cousin and her mom an aunt. Mom, how am I doing in the "ladylike" department?

"I'm glad you still recognize me. I'm not wearing nearly as much makeup as I usually do," Brooke said. She giggled a bit. She sounded so…normal to me.

I had to admit, I didn't even notice how well made up her face was when I first walked into the room. But when she pointed it out, I did see that she was wearing a touch of coverup and mascara. She looked pretty, with her red hair and green eyes. I could tell that most people might have turned running in the other direction if they ever met her in person, a little scared of her Christmas-color appearance and a matching cheery disposition, but I liked her when I saw her on TV, and I liked listening to her voice, even if the only place I ever heard her sing was on the radio. She was just breaking out onto the pop scene. Either way, she looked good, no matter how much makeup she was wearing.

I noticed my heart was still in my chest, though it felt like it was trying to fly out any second. I suppose that is what's called being starstruck, something I never thought in my whole life I would ever have the chance to experience. I wanted to be a singer, no doubt, so was it a good sign that now there was a professional singer in the house? "Wow, yeah...you can't tell at all...I wouldn't have known if you hadn't said anything." Thank God I finally did find my voice. Guess I wasn't slated to be starstruck forever, though I was still in shock.

"Well, looks like the girls are getting along just fine. Lina, let me show you the rest of the house..." Mom trailed off, waiting for a reaction from Mrs. Fulton, and winking at me as Mrs. Fulton followed her out of the room, leaving Brooke with me. Did she think this was my chance to make a new friend? I could see those were the inner workings of my mom's mind, even if she didn't tell me what she was thinking. I didn't know how I felt about that. Brooke seemed sweet, yeah, but it could have been fake sweet. For the first two minutes we just stared at each other, until it occurred to me that I was the host. Mom left, so that meant I was in charge, something I was definitely not used to.

I wasn't sure what to say or if it was even my turn. I mean, did being a good host absolutely mean that I went first? Sometimes I wished I could shut off my thoughts like a faucet and end this flow of superfluous ponderings. My brain was like a basin. Sometimes it just liked to fill up with ideas and worries. They would get caught in there and then stay, swirling around like the water in a stoppered sink. Then one day, when it got too full to hold in, the thoughts would flow out slowly, and there'd be nothing to stop them from draining.

I figured it might be too personal too soon to ask why she was staying with us, so the only thing I could come up with was, "Hey, so do you need help with luggage or unpacking or anything?"

That did the trick. We were finally free to roam the house and the yard. She had a suitcase in the trunk of her car. It looked like a really nice car, but then I'm kind of a bozo when it comes to cars. She saw me staring at it, so she patted the trunk and said, "Carwash." I was amazed that there were no paparazzi around, but then again, this was Bellemont; that was probably why she was here in the first place. I guess if my name were Brooke Fulton, I'd want to hide out in a nobody town, too.

"Oh, cool," I said. I was definitely not feeling cool, but I was trying to hide that. I guess that meant the car wasn't brand new or anything. It just looked that way. At least now the license plate made sense: B F were her initials.

She opened the trunk. I was kind of expecting the luggage to be big and bulky. Instead, there were two small suitcases and they both fit well inside the trunk. By this time I had so many questions I didn't know where to begin. Mostly I didn't want to offend her, and I wasn't even sure which questions were appropriate and which ones weren't. I even felt weird acting like this around her, like she was some kind of princess or something.

I didn't say anything as I lugged one suitcase and she lugged the other.

"So what's Bellemont like?" Brooke asked me this question with a smile, as if she asked regular, normal schoolgirls this question all the time.

As we walked up to the house together, pulling on the handles of the luggage, I told her in a voice that was as normal and regular as I could manage all about this little town, leaving out parts about school, of course. She did, after all, ask about this town, not about me and my life. So no Revelation, no mention of how my life had been reduced to hanging out by myself in my room on Friday nights. I suspected she wanted to find something cute about this little place that she could tell all her pop-star friends when she got back home, to her real place of residence, wherever that was: New York, L.A.? If she was hiding from the paparazzi, she must have been hiding from one of those two cities. That was why I had to leave out the school parts—because while it was true you could hide away from the paparazzi in Bellemont, you couldn't avoid Hollywood when you stepped inside the halls of Serenity Creek High. I figured I'd do her a favor and skip that whole scene.

She nodded at the part when I told her about the Hoop, laughed at the part about Buns 'N' More being the social center of the town, and smiled at the part about

OIL IN THE WOK

Co~Z Monster being the coffee place where everyone hung out.

After I was done, I realized she had been politely silent the whole time, listening to me blabber on. I didn't know if she was genuinely interested in what I had to say, but it seemed that it was sufficiently entertaining that she didn't feel the need to ask any questions. I took that as a good sign, which surprised me at first. It had been a long while since I had a good feeling about anyone or anything. It would probably take a few days before I got down to the real reason she was hiding out in Bellemont and what happened to her dad, but for now, it was nice to know that at least one person in this house besides me now saw things from my perspective.

I helped Brooke set up in the guest room and then suddenly realized I still had to do my AP Bio! She said she'd be okay, that she'd manage, that she just needed me to tell her a bit of how the streets in the neighborhood

35

ran so that she could go jogging. I told her that would be fine, but she'd better not take long because it was almost time for dinner. Then I asked her if that would be okay. Who was asking whom for permission? And shouldn't Mom have been the one enforcing the rules? I mean, this wasn't my house. It was hers, especially if she finally got Dad to move out. They were basically "separated," but still living together. That part I left out also. I didn't think we were quite that close yet. She'd soon find out, though; nothing in this town stayed a secret for long. Let's just say my parents' broken marriage was not on the top of my "things to discuss with friends" list. Some days, I didn't even know whether I should believe the rumors or my own dad. Most would say that I led a pretty strange life, but it was really quite simple: trust no one.

Brooke was amazingly fast at changing into her sports bra and jogging shorts. I was sitting at my desk, poring over my notes on osmosis when I looked up and saw her running along the street past my window. I still couldn't believe that we had a living, breathing diva in our house. It was like Darwin just discovered a new species of birds or something. I still wanted to know the true story. It was a story I might never get, even with her so close by, but the idea is what kept me curious.

Our house was going to change—for worse or for better, it was not going to stay the same. That thought was already finding its way into the basin, creeping in stealthily, almost unnoticed. It snuck up on me while I was memorizing the process of self-pollination. It crawled on my skin, up my back as I filled in the answers to the questions on the review packet with a blue ballpoint pen. It was inevitable, this change, and the first thing that was going to change was the bathroom. I knew it in my heart, I knew it in the air that filled my lungs, and the thought was there, caught in my hair at night as I tried to fall asleep on my bed. The oil was just getting hot.

It had been a week now, and Mom said that Lina said that her daughter did not wish to go to school with me yet. Why Brooke couldn't have just told me that herself, I had no idea. In fact, I hadn't seen her around much. I didn't even know how her mom and she got along with just the one car and one room. They basically shared everything with us, and our bathroom cabinet was getting more and more crowded. Amazingly, we managed to squeeze all of Brooke's female stash in my bathroom and jammed all of Lina's stuff in Mom's bathroom. Somehow, it worked out. Dad was the only lucky one in this area— since he was the only male, he'd gotten a bathroom all to himself. Yeah, all I could say was, it wouldn't have been fun for the Fultons to share with Dad. He was taking this all pretty well, considering there was now twice as much estrogen under one roof as there was before. He really had no choice as Mom was set on getting a divorce and he would be moving out soon anyway.

It was a Wednesday afternoon and I had just parked my car in the driveway, the only one there at the moment because Mom was at her office and Brooke had taken her car out for a spin somewhere, having dropped her mom off at the nearest spa, or so I heard. It was one of those rare moments when I had the whole house to myself. I couldn't even begin to describe how excited I felt as soon as I realized this beautiful phenomenon. I was almost inspired to make it to the Hoop. Almost, but I didn't go. Instead, I decided to revel in my solitude and fill out college applications. Yes, they were all state schools for now because I still wasn't sure about pursuing a music career, or even a full-fledged art career. Heh, ironic considering our new condition, but nevertheless I felt really happy and college applications were the first thing on my list of things I needed to do.

I had to hand it to Brooke. In the brief time that she had spent in Bellemont, so far she hadn't been recognized by one fan. Not one person knew who she really was. She'd been exceptional with her disguises. Usually it just consisted of a hat and sunglasses, but she pulled it off really well. I guess it was because no one in their right mind expected to see Brooke Fulton in the flesh—and in Bellemont of all places. We were so used to seeing celebrities only on TV that it never crossed our minds that maybe one of them might visit us in our solitude. But one thing about her hadn't changed at all—she had only been here about a week and she had already been asked out by three different guys. Lucky her! It didn't really bother me that much, though, surprisingly. I mean, some girls my age, like Karen and Serena, lived for that kind of thing. It would have been cool if some guy ever asked me out, but I didn't need to keep tabs on who was dating whom. I'd be flattered to know that someone was interested in me, but at the same time, even if no one were interested in me, I'd be cool with it.

From what I could tell, Brooke was pretty normal. That both scared and relieved me. I mean, I'd heard it said many times that people were not always what we expected or what we imagined them to be, but I always pictured her as your typical popular girl at school. Not like I'm good at reading people or anything—just take one look at how great I was at picking my best friends and you'll know. But for some reason, I'd always thought I *knew* Brooke, even though my judgments were based solely on what I saw of her in the media. She might have been the most distant

41

person I knew in my life, but to me, I knew the girl behind the voice on the radio. She was and always would be just Brooke.

Just Brooke liked to get up at five o'clock every morning, including Saturdays and Sundays. She said that showers woke her up better than coffee ever did. She did a brief Starbucks stint when she first started recording her debut album, then right after her sophomore album, *Babble On*, was released, she quit drinking coffee of any kind and started her getting-up-at-the-crack-of-dawn routine. That meant no more white chocolate mochas or vanilla lattes or anything else that came in a short, tall, grande or venti size. Good for her. I had heard somewhere that it's bad to drink coffee at a young age. Stunts your growth? Maybe I heard that from Isaac…not sure…

Just Brooke liked to do Pilates after she took a shower and grabbed a granola bar for breakfast, though she usually skipped breakfast altogether. She didn't really like

42

drinking milk so the answer to "Got milk?" would be "no" for her. She did like a good cheeseburger with the friedest fries possible though. I was glad, because I had to admit, I totally thought she was a salad girl. Those girls annoyed me. She also didn't throw up after every meal like she was the best dancer in the American Ballet Company or something. She was worried about her weight, but I think it's every girl's right to be interested in how much she weighs. It's like it's genetically wired into girls' minds that we have to be thin. But that didn't mean we had to starve ourselves. I mean, if your name was Brooke Fulton, I doubt you'd have to constantly worry all the time, at least not on purpose. All that dancing and working out had to be enough to burn off the few extra calories you might have eaten.

Just Brooke liked to read for hours. She could pick up a 500-page book in the morning and be on page 495 by dinnertime. She said it took her mind away. She loved to sing, but sometimes she just wanted to read. She liked to watch DVDs of old classics like *The Sound of Music* and *Sabrina*. The movies of today disgusted her, she said, unlike the elegance of the classics. There was too much "gross stuff." When I asked her what "gross stuff" was, she said everything the average teenage boy probably hid in his secret stash under the bed and then some. Oh, and besides "gross stuff," there were too many idealistic scenarios that would never ever happen in real life. Then I told her that that was why it was called a movie. I mean, *anything* can happen in a movie. That's the whole point. Chick flicks, she called them. They annoyed the heck out of her—she absolutely could not stand them.

It was really nice to think of Brooke Fulton as just Brooke.

The house was so peaceful it was kind of scary. I mean, it had been quieter lately anyway since neither Karen nor Serena came over anymore. Should I have been concerned that my only true friend of late was a pop star who had been walking around town incognito to avoid a massive fan attack and would probably be leaving sometime soon? I didn't know. Maybe it was nice not to have too many guests over at once and the only thing I had to worry about was how to keep Brooke's identity undercover. That was already enough to fill a whole plate.

It felt weird sitting there filling out a bunch of forms while there was no one home. I mean, on the one hand, it was nice because it was practically like a doggie treat to have so much space and quiet. But on the other hand, it meant something was up. Usually that meant there was going to be a huge change of some sort. And it was not always good. And I was never the first one to know.

After working on the applications for about an hour, I started feeling hungry. I walked down the hall and onto the tiles that lined our kitchen floor. I opened the door to our pantry and grabbed a Snickers, one of those kingsize bars. I hadn't eaten anything since I got home and now I was starving. Mom always said that sometimes when you're really hungry, all you need is a little bit of sugar. It would give you a boost of energy and then—whoosh!—you were not so hungry anymore. Well, whether eating chocolate was going to keep me from keeling over or it was the placebo effect that was going to do the trick, I was at the point where it didn't really matter. I just needed something to eat.

I was a few feet from the front door and just as I took my first bite, I could hear the key turn in the lock. In walked Brooke, with Mrs. Fulton in tow. I nearly dropped the candy bar on the floor. Oh, it was Brooke, but it was not *the* Brooke Fulton. Her hair was blonde!

"Ta-da!" Mrs. Fulton presented her daughter in the doorway like she was the main entrée sitting on a silver platter. Then she pulled out an empty box of hair dye.

I couldn't contain myself. I ran over to read the box. It was from Revlon. It was Light Ash Blonde. Oh, so that was the color she chose. But why?! Somehow I think I knew the answer to that question…

The next day Brooke declared that she wanted to go to school with me. To Serenity Creek High. To blend in and catch up with her schoolwork. She wanted to sit next to me in all my classes, but she was going to audit them, meaning she'd sit in on them without taking a grade. She just wanted to know what it was like to be normal again, the way things were before she became Brooke Fulton. Now that her hair wasn't red anymore, gone were the sunglasses and the hat. And the hoodies.

And her identity as a singer. She was now Sally Hunter, best friend of Amber Yang. From now on that was what I had to call her. Sally Hunter with the light ash blonde hair. She wanted to get blue contact lenses, but Lina drew the line at strange eye colors. Still no one had recognized who she was, so Lina figured her daughter would be fine with just a different hair color.

I was stuck. Now I *had* to tell her about the Hollywood scene. I tried to warn her that although no one had heard of a Sally Hunter before, my school was known for talking. It would just be ironic for a girl who was desperately trying to avoid a high-profile life for the moment to walk right into the midst of it, here, in Serenity Creek High, the least serene place I knew. As I began to tell her all about the wonderful social hierarchy at our illustrious high school, she put her left hand on my left arm, looked me dead in the eye, and interrupted my spiel with, "Amber, it's going to be okay. Whatever happens, happens. It doesn't matter if I don't follow your school's rules. It doesn't matter if I fall flat on my face. I've just got to go to school."

When she put her hand on my arm like that, something shifted in the way I perceived her. Maybe it was something in the atmosphere or in my heart or what, but I started to feel warm and fuzzy inside. I still remembered the day my seventh-grade Social Studies teacher described "warm and fuzzy" to the class. My teacher, what-was-his-name? I forget, but I will always remember that he said warm and fuzzy was like drinking a hot chocolate when it was freezing outside or when someone gave you a compliment or said something that made you feel good inside and you got all tingly. I definitely felt tingly.

Warm and fuzzy felt good. It wasn't that I had never felt this tingly before—I had. It was just that it took me by surprise because I hadn't felt like this in a long time. Maybe it was because it had been a while since I had a friend, but that spark was not something I expected and it just felt good.

Sally Hunter needed a wardrobe change. If she wanted to be normal, she had to dress normal. So Sally and I hit the mall that Friday. And again on Saturday. Let it be known that nothing else in the world can bond two girls together better than shopping at a mall. We did not leave Serenity Creek Mall until Sally had all the gray cardigans she could handle and all the black boots she could walk in.

On Monday we strutted the halls of Serenity Creek High. Okay, more like Sally Hunter strutted and Amber Yang sauntered. Obviously Brooke had adjusted faster to her new wardrobe and acknowledged that change in the atmosphere faster than I had. Nevertheless, I thought the two people who couldn't have been more surprised upon seeing this new pair walking down the hallway would be Karen and Serena, who, after giving us mean looks, especially me, immediately began whispering in each other's ears. Sally Hunter had officially entered the building.

I tensed up. I couldn't help it. My heart started pounding, and not because I was nervous or anything. I could hardly part my lips to utter anything coherent, let alone breathe. There was so much I wanted to say, yet at the same time I didn't want to say anything at all if that was even possible. My tongue felt stuck and I could feel my face burning up already. I was angry and I didn't know how to express myself without punching their faces in. Brooke must have had a sixth sense or something because she noticed right away that something was up. "Ignore them," she whispered brusquely. I was amazed. She didn't know them, but she could tell they were bothering me. And she knew exactly what to say so that my tensed-up mouth could finally relax. In my mind I knew that some day I'd have to explain Karen and Serena, possibly even Revelation, but for now I was grateful to have a friend who had my back again.

I didn't know if I really wanted to reveal anything to Brooke just yet, but I didn't have much choice since we were already here, right in the midst of the Hollywood scene at Serenity Creek High. That day she shadowed me just like she said she would, and surprisingly no one recognized her. It never ceased to amaze me how she managed the normalities of the teenage existence with such ease. Every teacher was nice about her auditing the class. In fact, most of them couldn't seem to remember the last time anybody ever audited their class. I got a few stares from people, but it was all right. Nothing too out of the ordinary—that is, no more attention than I had been getting ever since the night of Revelation. I was sure they were wondering who this new blonde girl was and why I wasn't seen with Karen or Serena by my side anymore.

When we got to Mr. Kurt's health class, I don't know why, but I started to get nervous. I guess I was afraid that Brooke would find out about Isaac. But why would I be afraid of that? That was the real question and not one I could have easily answered.

I sat down at my desk, and Brooke, who was now Sally, pulled up a chair next to me. And there was Isaac, sitting at his usual desk at the usual table, which is not where he had to sit when he was working on a group assignment with me. So far, so normal. I tried to calm down a bit and catch my breath. (Was it sad that I was losing my regular inhaling and exhaling ability over a stupid upperclassman boy, afraid a complete stranger to this town would see right through me and figure out how I really felt about him, which at this point, was unclear even to me?) What did all this superfluous excitement mean anyway? That I wished I had a girl friend whom I could gossip with about boys? After all, there was nothing outstanding about the way Isaac looked. He was, for the most part, unnoticeable. I mean, I liked it when he smiled—he was always so serious—but apart from that, there was nothing special. Maybe, with any luck, Sally wouldn't notice him. I wasn't sure if that included Brooke.

I tried not to stare. I tried not to turn my head. I tried not to peek. I could not let Sally see. It was working! At first, Isaac really kept up a good appearance of someone who didn't pay attention to any new changes going on around him. But when Sally finally sat down, he glanced over at us, just like the rest of the following eyes in the class. I guess he was just curious as to who this new girl was and what exactly she was doing with me. When I looked up at his face, he looked away just in time. At first, Sally didn't notice this exchange—we kept it up throughout the duration of the class. It was a good thing Mr. Kurt wasn't going over anything too hard to remember because I found that it wasn't easy to catch Isaac's glances while listening to the health teacher go on with the day's lesson.

Unfortunately, by the end of class I was sure Sally had caught on, especially with the number of times Isaac lifted his eyes to observe us from across the room. The whole way while driving home, she wouldn't stop badgering me about him. In fact, this was the most energetic I'd seen her in days. She usually didn't show too much emotion, a lot like Isaac's facial expressions—or lack thereof. I tried pointing this out to Sally to illustrate the flaw in her observation that this "cute guy" had a "thing" for me, but I don't think it worked. I wanted to kick her out of the car, but seeing as how I had to keep my right foot on the gas and my hands on the steering wheel, that was kind of difficult.

If there was one thing I hated, even more than the events that unfolded on the night of Revelation, it was when girls overanalyzed things, especially mixed signals from guys. I personally believed that there were no such things as signals, let alone mixed signals. Yeah, sounded harsh, but it was the truth! If Isaac was looking over at me, he was probably just looking over at Sally because she was new. Everyone's head always turns, naturally, when the door to a classroom opens in the middle of a lecture or when there's a lot of commotion in the hall or when some new girl comes in to class unannounced! There were no hidden meanings—the tilt of the head in a girl's direction is by coincidence. Coincidence that she's sitting right by the door or the source of the interruption. When girls start to overanalyze every single head nod, wave of the hand, wink of the eye, and whatever else there is that is analysis-worthy, that's when the problems begin and the drama-free days are over. Girls will start chatting about these so-called signals, and then one girl gets superexcited over every move her crush makes when really he's just being nice and helping her to pick up the pencil she accidentally dropped onto the floor. Go figure. The phenomenon never ceased to baffle me.

I tried to ignore Sally's deductions about what Isaac's glancing over at me meant, but it was hard. For a girl who wanted to take a break from her singing career she sure knew how to use her voice! Still, I made an effort to focus on the good things. Sally might have been loquacious, but she knew how to keep a girl company and distract her from the darkness of her mind.

By the time Friday rolled around, I was astounded that everything had run basically very smoothly. I mean, unlike what I was expecting, Sally Hunter made one studious, not to mention courteous student, who followed me without much questioning and didn't check her hair and makeup in a compact mirror every two seconds like a lot of the girls at school did, including Karen and Serena. I had to admit, I guess I hadn't gotten over the whole, omg!-there's-a-diva-living-in-my-house syndrome as quickly as I thought I would. But then again, who knew how long that was gonna take, right?

Brooke was amazingly good at her new double life. A little too good. Not that I was complaining or anything. She asked my teachers for copies of everything so that she could do the homework along with me. They readily agreed, never having taught a student who was so eager to learn before, especially not one who wasn't even taking the classes for credit. But they did also specify that we were to do our own work and not share answers with each other. Yeah, that sounded more like it.

It was the end of health class and Mr. Kurt had just dismissed us. Sally and I grabbed our stuff and started walking out the door. Just as we got out into the hall, she brought up Isaac. Only this time, she kept nudging my shoulder to tell me that he had been looking at me again. I had definitely had enough, so to change the subject, I announced that I was going to the Hoop after school let out for the day. I asked her if she wanted to come with. As she paused before answering, I felt her nudge my shoulder again. Apparently Isaac was walking right behind us. She chose that moment to answer loudly and exaggeratedly, "Yes, Amber. I'd like to go to the Hoop with you after school today."

I gave her a look that I hoped conveyed, omg! could you *be* any more obvious?! A sneaky feeling crept into my heart right at that moment. It seemed that Sally was planning a bit more than I had suspected. Why she wanted to hook me up with Isaac, I had no idea though. Nah. That couldn't be. She couldn't really be thinking about that. I mean, what did Isaac and I have in common, besides health class? We were polar opposites! He was Mr. Opinionated and I was Miss Doll, there for show, not for sharing thoughts. It was amazing. For a girl who really didn't care about signals, let alone mixed signals, I sure put a lot of thought into this whole couple thing.

When we finally pulled into the parking lot of the Hope Court, with me fighting the urge to push Sally out of the car, I almost fell over after I slammed the car door shut. There was Isaac. Shooting free throws. Did this guy have any more surprises up his sleeve? No, this had to be a coincidence, I thought. He just happened to be at the same place at the same time. There couldn't be any other explanation because there were no such things as signals. No such thing. Or maybe it was all in my head. Sally had told one joke too many about me and Isaac, Isaac and me. How many different combinations could there be?

Just then, out of nowhere, Sally tackled me—with tickles. She pushed me onto the grass and uttered over and over again, "You know you want him." I tried to get her off of me, but I couldn't stop giggling, which was bad because even though I didn't care about Isaac in *that* way, it was still embarrassing to be attacked like that by another girl. I mean, come on! How would that look to *any*one who had been passing by?

It was moments like these when I got not only a sudden attack of the giggles (because I was nervous) but also a sudden attack of mixed emotions. I know, seemed strange. The girl who didn't believe in mixed signals believed in mixed emotions. Well, it was true.

On the one hand, I really felt self-conscious. I didn't want Isaac to get the wrong impression. I mean, anything could have been going on in that teenage boy's mind of his, some of which I did not even have the imagination for. On the other hand, I really wondered why I should care about what Isaac thought anyway. If I cared, did that mean I liked him? And if I didn't care, did that mean I only thought of him as a friend or not as anyone special at all? Was he just the senior guy in my health class? Or was he the *cute* senior guy in my health class? It was funny sometimes how one word could change the whole entire meaning and description of one person and how you felt about that person.

Turned out, though, this time my attack of the giggles didn't matter because Isaac wasn't paying attention to our little tickle-fest. Thankfully. It was a good thing either way since my brain couldn't figure out how it felt about the whole situation. Now I didn't have to worry about it. Well, I may have been a *little* disappointed. But that didn't mean anything.

After a while, another car pulled up. Amidst the laughing and scrabbling around on the grass, trying to figure out what we were going to do next and how much I wanted to share with Brooke (she was only Sally while we were in school) about the Hoop, I noticed out of the corner of my eye, a group of guys stepping out of the car and going up to Isaac. Isaac stopped dribbling for a sec and hugged the ball to his hip. They exchanged their guy handshakes, complete with fist bumps full of "hey mans", "sups", and "dudes", and then one in particular stopped to ask Isaac a question before tilting his head in the direction of the grass Brooke and I were on.

Wait, was I imagining things? I really hoped it wasn't one of those things that only seemed to happen in my head. It went by so fast I barely had time to process what was going on. Luckily, Brooke hadn't noticed. In another sec, one of the guys had challenged Isaac to a pickup basketball game. As they got more and more into it, for the first time since I started going to the Hoop, I wasn't focused on *playing* the game. I was focused on *watching* the game. And I was trying really hard not to focus all my attention on a particular someone. It wasn't easy. Every few dribbles of the ball or swish of the net and my eyes would somehow find their way back to him. I didn't even know why. I had never seen Isaac at the Hoop before, but it was hard not to notice now. He was *good*. I wondered why he wasn't on Varsity at school, then I wondered where he must be practicing to get so good. Then I wondered why I was so interested! Brooke didn't notice; she seemed to be content to be a normal teenager for a change. And just for that, all of the giggle attacks, tickling antics, mixed emotions, warm fuzzy feelings, and anything else that had to do with the craziness that is called being a teenage girl suddenly disappeared.

We didn't stay to watch which team won. I wasn't even sure they were keeping score. I could tell Brooke wanted to stay, but she was really gracious about it and kept that bit of information to herself. We were in that mood, though, that was for sure.

"That mood" was that special frame of mind, only pertaining to teenage girls, when a girl feels chipper. But not just usual chipper. More like the excited, carbonated, warm explosive kind of cheeriness that you taste when you take your first sip of soda. Giddy. Giddy chipper. A happiness that verges on vertigo, yet freeing at the same time. When us girls get into this state of mind, there's no telling what we may do. We feel like singing our favorite love song at the top of our lungs. We feel like dancing. We feel like turning up the jam. We feel like having a sleepover, complete with feather pillow fights and jumping like crazy on mattresses. A lot of these can be done by ourselves, but it's even nicer when we have other girls around us for moral support—you know, just in case one of us ends up in jail or something. And oh yeah, popcorn. There's gotta be lots and lots of popcorn. Don't ask.

It was Friday night. Brooke and I were definitely both in that mood. I think watching any kind of sports game can get a person in a temporary high or chipper state of mind. But to get into "the mood" was not just about the sports competition hype. It was also a feeling that two girls had accomplished something together. I had helped Brooke get through one whole week of school with me, with her passing as light ash blonde Sally Hunter. Not one person recognized her as Brooke Fulton. *The* Brooke Fulton. Which I suppose is what she wanted all along since she found her safe haven here in Bellemont. We were such a small town, everyone had the same dentist.

OIL IN THE WOK

His name was Dr. Minder and he liked to take polaroids of his patients' 100-watt smiles after the regular cleanings by his hygienist. The pictures immediately got tacked to the bulletin board. When you walked in, you saw dozens of bright smiles covering the wall.

We were going to have a sleepover, just the two of us, with lots of popcorn. It wasn't planned, but given the mood we were in, it was simply inevitable. It was time for a celebration. Brooke was all for it. I think she wasn't just in "the mood"; she was truly happy. I was glad to be a part of it, and I just felt like singing and dancing on the bed. So when we got home, that's what I did while Brooke went into our kitchen and started making microwave popcorn. She might not have had any ideas about how to use the stove, cutting board, or knife, but she sure knew how to work the microwave. It must be an essential skill of a pop star or something because I have never seen anyone that excited to go heat up something edible in my whole life. Of course, I was only sixteen, so that could explain it. It didn't matter. What mattered was having popcorn because there was no doubt that junk food was high on the list of the necessities for a spontaneous sleepover.

I didn't use the iPod this time. This time I wasn't spending Friday night alone, brooding over my zero friendships and the never-ending Iris and Mark saga. I didn't know how long it would be before Mom and Dad finally realized how much they loved each other, but I didn't feel like finding out that night. I just hoped they wouldn't start biting each other's heads off while Lina and Brooke were staying in the house. I switched on the stereo in my room and blasted some music. The station was Z103.5, probably the second most listened to station among my peers, but it was definitely the number one station to my ears.

OIL IN THE WOK

If I ever became a singer, I'd be the kind who liked to sing with her hands. I wasn't your typical, pick-up-a-brush-and-use-the-handle-as-a-mic kind of gal. Nope. Leave that to the movies and other cliché Hollywood scenes. I liked to sing with my face, my hands, and my voice. It seemed simple if you really thought about it, but I didn't use a mic. A microphone always looked intimidating to me. Okay, so maybe not intimidating, but I'd feel real stiff if I had to use one. It would be like a ballerina trying to do a pirouette with a long rope attached to her waist. I found singing under the most natural conditions allowed me to be free to express how the lyrics to a specific song made me feel.

I guess I got the affinity for all things natural from Mom. She was a big fan of natural remedies, which was ironic, considering she made a living out of altering celebrities' faces with every unnatural chemical imaginable. And okay, I was not a plastic surgery expert, so maybe I didn't know all the dirty details, but the point was going under the knife was not exactly the most natural thing you could do to keep yourself looking young and fresh. That much I did know.

I wasn't sure how Brooke the pop-star diva was going to react to my choice of music. As a singer she might have been really particular. I did know that if Karen and Serena and I were all still on speaking terms, they'd love the music that was blasting from my stereo just then. That was the thing with certain memories. They popped into your head when you were least expecting them, sometimes when you didn't mean to conjure up any memories at all. For me, one thing always led to something else that happened in my past. I'd see a helmet and that would suddenly remind me of the time in fourth-grade art class when we had to make our own King Tut tomb replica using sandpaper, construction paper, glitter pens, markers, colored pencils, staples, and cotton balls for stuffing. Somehow the helmet would lead me to that particular memory. It was weird how at times I'd get a detailed image and other times I'd get a vague one. And good or bad, I'd see one thing and start thinking about something totally different. I guess that was normal, though. It also probably could be traced back to Mr. Frasca. At the beginning of the year last year, he made us all take this special test that basically asked us certain questions to find out how we liked to study. There were no right or wrong answers. At the end of the test, we learned how we, well, learned best. I found out I was a visual learner. That would explain a lot. It sure explained why I couldn't concentrate in class when the teacher would drone on and on while writing stuff on the blackboard. It explained why I could only get something when I looked at diagrams and pictures in the textbooks by myself at home. My brain always wanted to create, always wanted to look at things differently than everybody else, and always, always, always wanted to jump out of the classroom.

"So this is what the Serenity Creek High kiddies listen to, huh?" Brooke asked, teasingly.

"Yep, and mostly I listen to it," I responded, unfazed.

Just then, "Jumpin', Jumpin'" by Destiny's Child came on and we both started singing at the top of our lungs while swinging our hips to the beat. Karen and Serena popped into my head again. In our sweet, uncomplicated past, the all-Chinese Destiny's Child used to sing one Destiny's Child song or another on our way over to Co~Z Monster. It was our thing before the group split up. While singing "Jumpin', Jumpin'" with Brooke, though, I tried hard not to think of my ex-BFFs. I knew there was no way I'd forget the past, but I wanted some new memories. I desperately wanted some new memories.

It was great. Then the commercials came

on and Brooke started singing something else in place of the Geico announcement blaring through the speakers. "Isaac loves Amber," she repeated over and over again.

Oh no! She wasn't starting with that again! If there was anything I hated as much as girls overanalyzing, it was the teasing about crushes, which I guessed qualified as overanalyzing anyway. If we aren't sure about our relationships with certain people, especially when boys are involved, then we shouldn't advertise it or make up something that is totally not true. It's just not right. But what can you do? I didn't know what to say to stop it. I never knew how to stop that kind of teasing. I mean, sure, it bothered me, but it was not the worst thing that could happen to me. Not by a long shot. So all I did was say one "Na-uh!" and left it at that. After all, a girl could let anything slide when she was in "the mood."

I had been wondering how long it would take before I had to bare all to Brooke. I mean, no matter what, we had agreed that Sally was not to know too much. And what she did know, she was to keep a secret. But it looked like the time for explanations was drawing near.

This was not going to be an easy feat, but I did warn her before we got started on this biz. Maybe that's just the way it was for me—always knowing beforehand that what I wanted to embark on was going to be a difficult task and there was a good chance I'd fail, but I always wanted to go through with it anyway. Like I deliberately set myself up for failure. Did that make me a masochist? In some twisted psychology of the mind and brain, maybe in the far, far, dark corners somewhere, like on a remote island or up in a black hole in outer space or something, did I secretly hide a side of me that actually enjoyed torturing myself? I mean, there was no doubt that in ancient Chinese history, servants endured copious amounts of physical and mental torture that would sometimes last for days and even weeks. Could it be that it was simply in my blood, as strange as that might sound? I mean, I hadn't officially checked or anything, but I was pretty sure that Yang was not a last name of Chinese royalty or anything. You probably wouldn't find the name Yang inside the Forbidden City. I didn't have any solid evidence or proof or whatever, but I didn't think I really needed any.

Either way, whatever the reasoning, in the back of my mind I was also aware that eventually Brooke was going to find out the truth one way or another. I just didn't want it to be so soon. It was going to be Thanksgiving in a couple of days and I really didn't want to ruin vacation time by discussing Revelation over turkey dinner. It promised to be a lengthy discussion, and I wasn't sure the one person I wanted to find out about it was a pop-star diva. Actually I hadn't been giving her enough credit. Ever since Brooke and Lina arrived, Brooke had been anything but a diva. And I didn't know whether it was because I was naturally drawn to people who turned out to be different from what I expected them to be or what it was, but it seemed like if I did want to talk about what happened, she'd be the one to tell it to. Maybe it was because she was from out of town. That had to be a big reason why I was able to trust her like I did. And God knew I hadn't been doing much of that ever since that infamous night.

On the Saturday night right before the Wednesday that school was going to let out for Thanksgiving break, Sally was invited out by some of Karen and Serena's new friends. It wasn't so long ago when I would have been

Sally, getting invited out with the popular crowd, but all that didn't matter now. No one at school wanted anything to do with me or my family. But Sally didn't know that and she thought it would be fine to invite me along.

"I just feel bad that I'm going out and you're gonna miss all the fun," Brooke was saying, sympathetically.

"Oh, I'll be fine. It's been a while since I've had the house quiet like this. I mean, *you* know how it is," I responded.

Brooke nodded. "Yeah, it probably will be nice. We'll have all break to spend together, won't we?"

I almost started laughing. When did we become a Hallmark commercial? Sally eventually left the house, just a little bit after Mom and Lina left for the salon to get their nails done—it was going to be Mom's first mani and pedi all at once and Lina wasn't going to miss it if her life depended on it. I had a slight feeling that was why Brooke

77

said yes to the invite. She was *not* going to tag along for the umpteenth time and coo over newly polished nails. She desperately needed to escape the watchful eyes of her mother. This might be normal for her as a pop star, but in a way, she was just being a normal teenager as well. All I said was, "All right, get outta here!"

Brooke fake-tackled me, then went back to her last-minute lip gloss check before heading out the door.

Yes! This was going to be my night! I was going to get a chance to hang out at home with just Dad around in the house. It was going to be peaceful, with no interruptions, just the sound of Dad grunting and the sewing machine running. I didn't know what project Dad was working on lately, but I could only hope it was something that would finally get his foot firmly in the door of the fashion world. Heck, if I felt inspired, maybe I could even help him out, but first things first. I had a night to spend in the quiet of the house, at least for a few hours. It's not like Mom and Lina were never coming back again, but a girl can indulge herself in the tranquility that is called an empty house.

No, I wasn't in "the mood." I was just daydreaming for a sec and it felt really good. It was Saturday night, it was almost time for Thanksgiving, and despite it all, I was feeling rather warm and fuzzy inside, exactly the way that my seventh-grade Social Studies teacher described it. *What* was his name again? (Note to self: look up old teachers' names and memorize them. It would also be helpful to really learn the names of the people who are in your life now so that later when you are thinking of them, you'll know their names. End note.)

I was feeling creative. Yes, I still had a bit of homework to do for the weekend, but it wasn't as much as the usual load. The teachers were being merciful and I was very grateful. I would probably end up doing most of it tomorrow anyway. It seemed to me that while Sundays might have been the days of rest for all those who believed in Jesus, for the rest of the world, especially high school students, Sundays were the days of catch-up. I didn't know what that meant for me and my afterlife and that of everyone else like me, but I did know that when I took time off from the stresses of school life, it happened to land on Saturday nights rather than Sundays.

This sudden attack of creative energy hit me, but I really had no idea what I wanted to *create* exactly. A picture? An ice sculpture? A painting? A poem? An invention? A new song? A short story? An experiment? A new hairstyle? A self-portrait? There were about a million and one things running through my head at that moment. But I thought, deep down in the depths of my cold, cold, frozen heart, I knew there was one thing I had to do. I had to write a song. But the song couldn't be made up from lame lyrics. They had to be poetic. And the one way to do that was to first write a poem. These were going to be beautiful lyrics. Something the listener could take in and not something that people had heard a thousand times before. Original. What every artist out there aims for. My brain had a tendency to push the fast-forward button. I was not an artist yet. I just hoped to become a singer some day. I didn't even know for sure if I'd end up singing pop, but I did know that I enjoyed singing pop the most. Well, that was not really a fair judgment. I hadn't exactly tried out any other genre, so I couldn't really say I didn't like singing opera for example. A girl could dream, right?

I sat down at my desk like I always did when I had to do homework, but of course, the plan wasn't to work on homework at all. I started to listen to the sewing machine hammering on in the basement. At first it was just the sounds of a machine. Just like any other machine, it sounded repetitive, thud-

thudding as the needle moved up and down, drawing thread in and out of the fabric. But after a while, they weren't just sounds anymore. They were beats. Not the beats of a drum; more like a metronome, keeping time. The beats that reached my ears from this sewing-machine metronome would keep the song steady, giving it rhythm, whatever the lyrics I ended up writing.

Bit by bit I listened to the hammering of the needle point and the grunting noises coming from Dad, and I picked up a ballpoint pen and a blank piece of loose-leaf paper. First, I started imagining some sort of tune. Just any kind of music that could possibly go along with this new beat I'd discovered. Then, I started bobbing my head to the beat. Slowly, a melody started to form. Now, I knew many music geniuses at this point would have already figured out what major it was in, what key, time signature, and so on. But I was not a music genius, so the best I could do was start humming a few bars. I wanted to write lyrics, not sheet music, for now, and I figured humming was enough accompaniment for me to do that.

It wasn't really working.

Songwriting was definitely harder than it looked. I supposed I wasn't a complete natural, but if given words to an already existing song, I could usually sing them and pick it up after listening to the song a few times. I wondered if that counted for something. Did every singer have fresh talent before becoming a singer, or did some have what I had: a good ear with a matching good voice that corresponded to the notes on the page? I mean, there was no real way to know for sure, unless...

The obvious answer to my woes was staring me right in the face and I hadn't noticed all this time! But the question was, did I want to risk telling her my life's plan? Granted, she wasn't having too much trouble keeping her double identity a secret, but how much can one girl handle really? Could she take on more confidential information? Especially the kind where it might involve someone's future career? Man, I sounded ridiculous! For an indecisive girl, I sure was sensitive about a lot of things. Maybe it had something to do with my hermitlike existence. This just wasn't healthy.

I didn't know what time she would be getting home tonight, but my best bet was it couldn't be too late or she would end up crashing at someone's place for the night. Lina could be a cool mom sometimes. She told her daughter that she'd either get picked up when she and Iris were on their way home or she'd have to sleep over at a friend's for the night. She wanted her back in one piece, no matter what. Wow. Just wow. Mom would never let me do that. Even back in my "crazy" days when Karen, Serena, and I would crash over at each other's pads all the time, my mom didn't like it. But it was our escape, our little thing to get over whatever unhealthy thoughts were creeping into our brains. It helped whenever we felt like we needed a support system. Only now, looking back on those times, I see they were so fake.

My creative mood had slumped a bit, but I wasn't losing all hope. I mean, I was just starting out, right? There shouldn't be any pressure to actually produce the whole song already. That was hoping for too much too fast. A hit song, if not written by a professional (well, not yet at least), could take anywhere from a couple of hours to a couple of months. I mean, even if I finished it, it'd still be like a rough copy. No hopes of it being a smashing success right off the bat. Anyway, right then it was hard to even measure how good it was with no one's opinion except for mine.

Songwriting, like all kinds of writing, could be frustrating. I just hoped the end product turned out good, or at the very least, passable for a song. If it smelled like a winner, then I'd be as happy as a bumble bee.

So I tried something else: I got up out of my seat and started to dance. I didn't know if dancing would work any better than humming, but I knew that I had to give it a shot. No pain, no gain, right? It was such a classic statement, but I had to remind myself every now and then.

"I am dan-cing…to this be-at…that I don't know…" I started to sing. They weren't real lyrics, but it was a start.

"I fe-el like a sewing mach-ine…"

I realized that my words weren't making much sense, and it was sounding a lot like describing what was happening in the moment. But on second consideration, it was a lot like telling a story. And isn't that what songwriting is all about? We want to tell a story, whether it's about love or life or something else, it doesn't matter. But there's always some sort of background story that helps to compose the words to the song. At least, that's what it seemed to me. Now as far as pop music was concerned, I knew that most of the songs were about love or had some sort of love story as part of their backdrop. If there's one thing everyone could relate to, it was love.

At the moment, though, I was far away from wanting to write a song about love.

Starting from scratch was going to be a daring move, but it was a risk I was going to have to take. Above all, I wanted to be original. I was certain that there was no way I wanted to pen lyrics that were so trite that you couldn't tell the difference who sang what anymore. At the same time, I really wanted my song to have a nice beat, just like all the Destiny's Child songs we liked to listen to. I knew they probably weren't exactly classified as pop, but it seemed to follow the same basic format. Oh, if I could have I probably would have sat down with the band members and had a good ol' chat and fire away with questions about how they got their first song, blah, blah, blah.

I was right in the middle of figuring out what words would go best with the new beat that I was dancing to when I looked up and I saw Brooke staring at me from the open doorway.

I froze.

Instead of her usual cheery self, she had this look on her face like she wanted to murder someone. She was still dressed up to party, the way she looked when she left the house. Seeing her now had two effects on me. At first, I was definitely wondering about the look on her face and whether I should be concerned or not. Then, I was thinking about how easily she assimilated herself into living under our roof. She basically could walk in and out with ease like she was me.

OIL IN THE WOK

At some level I was thinking, had Brooke taken over my place?

"Is it true?" she accosted me. When I didn't answer right away, she continued, "This is what you want for your future?"

The words hung in the air between us like a bowling ball hanging by a thread between our faces, waiting to drop or destroy the room.

She knew. That's all I could think about. And if they told her about the singing, I was sure they told her the rest of it, too. Somehow in one night, all the secrets were out. All my secrets, everything I had worked really hard to hide from everyone, were revealed. Brooke Fulton knew.

She knew. Revelation was not something I wanted people to know about, even though I was aware some people at school had heard. I mean, they had to, but I figured if I didn't talk to anyone about it, it could be like it never happened. Like ignoring the big yellow elephant standing in the middle of the room that everyone knew was there, yet pretended not to notice. I just didn't want to have to deal with it. I didn't want to be reminded all the time. That was the bottom line.

Yet, she knew. Brooke Fulton now knew everything. Blew my cover in one night.

Maybe I was being dramatic thinking these thoughts, but in severe cases, in my book it was okay to be dramatic.

I stopped dancing. I stopped writing. I looked at the girl staring at me. While we had worked really hard to keep her identity hidden, she had managed to uncover mine in just a few weeks. I couldn't believe it. She was not only taking over my place in this house, she was slowly exposing my secret dream! No one was supposed to know that I basically, well, wanted to be the next Brooke Fulton. My parents didn't know, and I planned on keeping it that way. Until I got somewhere with my singing, I really didn't want to reveal anything. I mean, I knew that there was no way that I could hide something this big forever, but I wanted to hide it from them for now, for as long as I could.

"Shh! Keep your voice down!" I said, trying my best to do the same. I let the bowling ball drop. Then I walked over to the door and shut it behind her. She didn't seem to mind. She seemed more concerned with unraveling the mystery that was called Amber Yang.

Luckily for me, Dad hadn't been paying attention to anything else since he immersed himself into his new project in the basement. The front door had escaped his attention and he made no sign of hearing it. If Brooke knew what was going on with me, fine, but I wasn't about to let everyone in the house find out along with her. That was the thing with timing—it was always off. You were either early or late, but never on time, right on the dot punctual. If you were, it happened maybe once in a blue moon. It was just like with love. You either fell in love right before the other person was leaving to start a new life somewhere else or you fell in love with someone right after you rejected him. If you fell in love at the exact same time that person fell in love with you, then you were very lucky. When it came to secrets, either you were ready to confess just when someone had already uncovered the truth, or right after you told someone not to tell, you found out everyone already knew. It was much like that Alanis Morissette song, "Ironic." And now it was my turn to experience it.

Brooke Fulton may not have been a diva, but she was a strong personality. I knew that she was going to put in much more than her two cents. And besides that, she was going to highlight the obvious that even I was starting to see: we desperately wanted to switch places, but we were afraid to let our parents know it. In a way it was ironic that Brooke, with all that training to sing in front of thousands of fans on stage night after night for weeks at a time, didn't possess the training to stand up for what she wanted the most for her life: to be normal. To go to school like a regular teenager and have plans to go to college and possibly more schooling after that. It just wasn't her thing to entertain as a singer for the rest of her life. I could see that was why she'd been hiding out from her celebrity at our house with her mom. It was obvious. I mean, granted someone else might have figured that out right away and not a few weeks later like I did, but let's face it, I hadn't exactly been myself in a long time. The old me would have just rolled with it. But the present me didn't roll with much of anything. Lately, I'd been annoyed with just about everything. It had made me cranky. Not pretty, but I had to admit it. That's what happens when you lose the trust of people you thought were your best friends in the world, including your mom and dad.

It was great that all this enlightenment was suddenly taking place in my head, but I just wasn't sure it was the right time to bare all and discuss, especially not with a pop star in hiding. Of course, it was possible people wouldn't even remember Brooke Fulton after she disappeared for such a long time from the public eye, but to be on the safe side, I really didn't feel like playing the dramaesque, gossip girl for the moment. I was comfortable being cranky. You should never force yourself to do something if you aren't comfortable and ready, right? It only makes sense to do what you have to do when the timing is right, right? At least it made sense to me that way.

Brooke was waiting for an answer from me now. I had kept her waiting. I tended to do that to people. I spent all this time thinking up all kinds of answers to a question, but I went through so many permutations that by the time I finally figured out the perfect thing to say, the other person had become so impatient they either walked away or started questioning me like crazy. Then I would go mute again, feel bad about keeping them waiting in the first place, and then feel like I needed to rethink my answer yet again. They were right when they said speech and writing are probably two of the hardest skills for human beings to learn.

Brooke was patient, though. I could tell she wanted me to speak, but she didn't rush me either. Maybe we connected on a singer-to-singer level or something or we just could read each other well, but I knew that my time was up. It was a hopeless cause. She definitely knew what was going on. It was now or never. I could keep quiet or I could spill. Either way she was about to launch the questions and extract it out of me if I didn't start talking soon.

"Yes," I replied solemnly, "this is what I want for my future." I kept it simple. Then I waited in silence to hear what she would say. She was bound to tell me how she found out everything. She was bound to tell me how she knew about my secret dream. It just had to happen that way. It wasn't right this way. I had to get some answers about how she knew what she knew—the rumors, Revelation, secret singing career—after everything my family had done for her.

"So you've been hiding from them all this time because of some stupid rumors they spread about you and about your dad?" Brooke asked, incredulously. "Is that it? Am I warm?" she pressed.

She looked to be on the verge of launching a bunch of questions at me at once, like I intuitively knew was going to happen. I was prepared for whatever she was going to do. I decided that right then and there.

"You felt ashamed, didn't you? So ashamed that you decided not to talk to anyone, not even Celeste…"

I nearly gasped right here. I suspected she knew the basics, the gist, I had no idea she even knew about Celeste! This was unbelievable.

"…or your mom or your dad. Am I right?"

I did nothing at first. Then I muttered, "Yes." I was grateful that she had not mentioned, *yet*, what those rumors entailed. Very grateful. So grateful I didn't know the words to describe how I felt. Celeste was good at that, so I usually left it up to her when she was still there for me. But now when I needed her most, she wasn't.

Such was the situation I found myself in the Saturday night before Thanksgiving break. Who knew? I wondered if this was the reason she had to come home early.

She hadn't done anything wrong, asking me all these questions, finding out all my secrets. It was a free country after all. I couldn't look at her. Brooke Fulton had slapped me in the face without lifting a hand.

I didn't want to talk about it, but she did. That's another thing with timing—when one person wants to talk, the other wants to be quiet. When one wants to be quiet, the other wants to talk. Or like missing roll call: the teacher announces your name, but you miss it somehow and then she marks you down as absent on her clipboard when you were sitting right there. Was that just me or was that how it went for everyone?

Brooke was now shaking me. I had zoned out. "Amber. Amber!"

I turned my head to look at her.

"Are you even paying attention to a word I'm saying? I want to help you!" Brooke exclaimed. She wasn't screaming in my face, but it sure felt like it. She was standing so close.

Was I frozen in time? This wasn't happening. I had been stuck in a rut for a few months now and this was no way to go on with my life, but still I was refusing to accept this fact and move on. What was wrong with me? Here was help staring at me right in the face, literally, and I wouldn't budge. What was I on if everything else in my life was functioning as usual? This part of my personality would take me years to figure out, with relatives I hadn't seen in years, with boyfriends, with friends from high school, with friends from college, with my parents, with new friends I met at work... It followed me everywhere. No matter what I did or who I talked to, I couldn't understand my ability to stay stuck in one mode like a rock in a river. Celeste had been the only one close enough to understand, but in the end, even *she* couldn't figure it out.

She didn't wait for a response from me. That was very wise of her. Instead, she pulled me into an embrace and hugged me. Yes, it was comforting, but I hated when people hugged me. I didn't know what they thought they were accomplishing by holding me tight. By surrounding me with their arms, did they really think they were solving something? Like my problems would all of a sudden melt away just because they were pretending that they understood and cared about what I was going through? What was the point of hugging, really? It accomplished nothing. Yet, I accepted the fact that finally, one person decided to help me out. That was better than the nothing that hugging accomplished. Only this time, Brooke's hug meant she cared.

Dad, after working all night, looked to be crashing on the cot in his workshop.

Mom and Lina were going to be walking through the front door any minute.

Brooke was ready to crash on the floor in my room.

And I wanted to disappear...now.... anywhere...it didn't matter...because I was simply not used to this kind of attention and care...from anyone. I didn't know exactly how much Brooke knew about what had happened to me a few months ago, but I could presume that she knew about Revelation. Much to my astonishment, I actually felt relieved. I had been hiding information from that night for so long that having Brooke find out felt much like confessing even though I hadn't said anything. It felt like getting something off my chest and that felt *good*.

At least once in a lifetime, everyone should have the chance to confess something. It doesn't have to be something that makes you feel bad or guilty or whatever, just something you haven't shared with anyone. It's really worth it to have that feeling of *good*. I don't know that you can get it anywhere else.

The thing is, we never discussed what happened directly. Brooke decided that that wasn't necessary. Her philosophy was anything that happened in the past stays in the past. Well, I didn't know what worked and what didn't, but following that philosophy had certainly worked for her. I knew there were a million girls out there who had wished to be in her shoes at some point in their lives. They would have given anything to be her for even just one day.

"All right, why don't we get some sleep tonight? We'll talk again in the morning, 'kay?" Brooke said in the most motherly fashion I'd ever heard her use. She wasn't really asking a question. She was telling me what to do. She expected me to listen. I didn't have an older sister, but at that moment, it seemed that if I had one, I'd want her to be just like Brooke.

The sewing machine stopped sounding. There was noise coming from the bathroom in the basement.

The front door opened for the second time that night. The clock read 11:00 p.m.

Two teenage girls were getting ready for bed.

These may not have been the typical sounds of a typical household on a Saturday night, but in a way, it probably was. I wasn't thinking about that of course, but I was thinking about how this all came to be. One thing was for sure: a new change was gonna come. Whether I was ready or not to accept this new change, only time would tell. But I didn't really have a choice now. Whatever the reason for pop star Brooke to enter my life, at this strange moment in time, I didn't know nor care. I was glad that I was finally going to move on with my life and get some much needed answers. The truth, even though I was too rock solid to admit to it, was that I just didn't know how to get on and here was the chance. It was time to get help, even though I had never asked for it before. I had never been one to seize the world with open arms, but I have never been one to shut the world out completely either. But after Revelation, things changed and I felt like it was irreversible. I didn't want things to be that way, but I didn't know what else I could do. I wanted to push the pause button. I needed an escape, and instead I found myself starting from scratch.

Recently my mother told me what happened to her the night Brooke found out everything. In a way, Iris had her own Revelation.

When Lina walked in first that Saturday night, she held onto Iris's hand. The two women walked across the foyer, one trying to recover from a meltdown. It had been a while since Iris found reason to break down like so, but that night she had crossed the threshold of her breaking point.

Lina and Iris had met in college. They had been friends for a long time, but after graduation they lost touch. They never forgot about each other though. Their friendship was the kind that I could only hope to have some day.

One day Lina was doing the dishes when she saw Dr. Iris Chen in the news. She was happy to see her old best friend from college doing so well, and she filed this piece of news in the back corner of her mind for future use. A few years later her daughter became a pop star, and Iris saw her friend Lina in the media as the stage mom. When Lina's daughter needed a cosmetic surgeon to remove a scar from her face, Lina thought of her good friend from college and in the blink of an eye, Brooke Fulton became a client of Dr. Iris Chen. For Iris, this opportunity to get back in contact with her old best friend was too great to pass up. The two felt lucky to have this time to spend together, and amidst everything that was transpiring, they finally had time to catch up on life. And as always, Iris found Lina very comforting during tough times like these, when her marriage seemed to be spinning out of control.

In the morning something had changed in the atmosphere.

It was Sunday. That much was true. I was still not friends with Karen and Serena. That was true as well. I had a headache. That was true, but not completely unexpected. I tended to get headaches whenever I had web-twisting, complex, heart-wrenching, emotional, personal life issues to deal with. A lot of times my head hurt as a result of a third party getting involved with said complicated issues. Sometimes I wondered if I had multiple personalities or something. Maybe I should have prayed. Nobody had asked me to do that in a long time, and I wasn't even sure I remembered how. What would Jesus have done? Was it really okay that instead of resting on Sundays, I did my homework?

When I woke up, I remembered I had homework to finish, Thanksgiving break was coming soon, thank God, and… what happened last night? It was a good thing Brooke didn't snore. I was able to get a good night's sleep even after the confrontation. But my head. Oh, my head. I lay awake for a while and didn't move until I heard Brooke finally stirring in her sleep. She seemed like she would be waking up soon, but I wasn't sure. It was already a little bit past ten o'clock and I was surprised. I usually slept in on Saturdays, not Sundays. When Brooke finally woke up, it was nearly half past. I was up and dressed and I thought this was the first time I'd seen her wake up so late. What did that mean? She didn't appear to have a headache like me, so that was a good sign. She didn't appear to want to murder anyone—also good. I felt relieved again. When she saw me, she said, "Finish your homework. This afternoon you start your lessons with me. You've got a lot to learn."

Whoa. For someone with such a laid-back persona, she sure understood military regimen. For the first time since this pop star had been staying with us, it occurred to me that I had never thought about the other parts of being a singer. It wasn't all concert performances and signing autographs. There had to be rehearsals, touring, interviews, dance routines, recording, and probably tons of other stuff I didn't even know about.

Well, whatever I had to learn, I was willing to give it a shot. You gotta do what you love and love what you do, right? And if that happened to take a few turns, dedication, and sometimes a stroke of luck, so be it.

That was the attitude I wanted to have that morning, but it was kinda hard with a headache and homework left to do.

"Tomorrow?" I asked.

"Today," Brooke responded without looking up.

OIL IN THE WOK

I decided maybe it wasn't a good idea to argue and left it at that. If things went my way, I wouldn't be doing homework for too much longer. Everything takes time to perfect, I thought, and if I have a professional with me now to help perfect my craft, who knows what I can do! Okay, maybe I was getting ahead of myself, but it's always nice to feel excited about embarking on a new project. The problem doesn't lie in the embarking. The problem lies in the finishing. Finishing what we start has probably been a problem for mankind since the beginning of the Ice Age.

Singing was going to be my ticket out of this rut. It was going to save me if nothing else could. But if that's how it was for me, how was it for Brooke? Wasn't her coming here a part of her being stuck right where she was, too? It seemed that we were in the same boat whether we wanted to admit it or not.

I was fortunate our four-day weekend was right around the corner. The teachers were really going light and hadn't assigned much for homework, as I checked my agenda when I pulled it out from my binder—a huge relief, if you asked me. However, I still wasn't finished with it in the afternoon when Brooke asked me how far along I was, hoping that I'd say I was done. I was conflicted—homework or singing lessons?—but finally I decided I'd just take a break and get back to it when Brooke was done with me. This was my dream on the line. If I didn't start making progress today, when would I ever? We agreed not to tell our parents what we were up to. Thankfully Brooke understood that much about keeping the parental units at bay.

For our first lesson, Brooke just wanted to hear me sing. She said this would allow her to better gauge how much practice I needed and what she could help me with.

It was kind of like a diagnostic test, like for the SAT or something. I usually preferred to sing along with CDs, but she didn't let me do that. She wanted to hear my natural voice, for obvious reasons. She said I could sing whatever I felt like singing. That was easy: I started with Destiny's Child. I was a bit nervous at first, feeling tense as I sang the first few lyrics, but as I kept going I found it relaxing. From then on, it was so easy to talk about the songs I liked, the songs I didn't like, and I could sing whatever songs popped into my head. I had never performed or practiced any of those songs, save Destiny's Child, for anyone before, but having Brooke there with me, our growing friendship only blossomed even more when I started my lessons with her. It really felt like an honor to be working with her, but it felt even better to have her on my side. A real friend on my side for a change. God only knew how much I needed that.

On Monday morning I was so tired I could barely lift my lids to keep my eyes open during class. Blame it on my first lesson with Brooke and the homework I had to finish for AP Studio Art, a self-portrait sketch. Mine was still, well, equivocal. But luckily, it was only supposed to be a sketch for now. I wasn't sure I was a truly defined person yet anyway. There was plenty of room for change, growth, and maturity. I only hoped by then the picture would be complete.

The bell had just rung to signal the end of classes. It was Wednesday finally and I was ready for the Thanksgiving break. Funny that a three-day week could go by slower than a regular five-day week. Brooke and I were officially best friends now, if there existed a course where two people could take a class and a test to see if they were like PB&J. I was comfortable enough to sing in front of her even when my voice would crack from time to time as I tried to reach the high octaves. This singing thing was tough! But most importantly, despite how hard it was, I was having fun and enjoying something for the first time. Like *really* enjoying what I did. That rarely happened. I wondered what that meant. I could draw, but only when I felt like it, which wasn't very often. I could do the schoolwork to pass all my classes, ace a few of them like Biology, but only because I had to do the work to graduate. I could sing all day and all night if given the chance.

Now still wasn't the time to announce to the world that I was going to be a pop singer. There was just no way it would

113

have been acceptable. And anyway, it was Thanksgiving—definitely not the time to drop a bombshell like this! I knew I had to find just the right moment, but as high school was coming closer and closer to the end and college fast approaching, I wondered how much time I really had. If I didn't do it soon, my world just might come tumbling down, like a boulder rolling down a hill.

We got home and I started running around the house like a crazy person. Dad was pulling an extra shift at Co~Z Monster. Mom was stuck at the office, calling her patients to remind them of their appointments one last time before the holiday. Lina was volunteering at an animal shelter, doing her best to keep a low profile. She figured talking to as few people as possible while her daughter was staying in town would help her daughter's career in the best way possible. It was a gift of mine to stay organized and on track with everyone's schedules.

The house was empty but for me and Brooke. She let me run around crazy for a few minutes before pulling me aside to remind me that we'd be rehearsing soon. Yep. It was official. Brooke was my coach and I was her pupil. Like I said, this singing business was tough. But it was time to get serious now or I never would, and then my life would just be a "woulda, coulda, shoulda," and I don't think anyone wants to look at her life like that. This meant that I couldn't have my old life back. I'd have to move forward and not look back. Getting right on track was going to be the only way I could let go of the past and put my best foot in the race ahead.

I realized that there weren't going to be days off. She really meant business. We'd be rehearsing tomorrow as well, even though it was a holiday. She said that the demo we'd be cutting had to be one hundred percent perfect. Yes, a demo! That was part of my plan and now she was going to help me turn it into reality! It was so exciting I could have jumped right out of my skin!

So as much as it hurt to lose my free time, I felt like I had to be willing to sacrifice some of that personal time so that I could follow my dream. Didn't we all have that drive? Didn't we all, deep down, no matter who we were, how famous we were, all want something bad enough that we'd sacrifice anything, do anything to get it or get to where we wanted to be? It made me wonder, what was that for Brooke Fulton? What did she ultimately want? Because it couldn't be what she was doing right now. I was sure her dream had never been to become a pop star, go into hiding, be normal again, and in the meantime, coach a nobody girl into a full-fledged singer.

OIL IN THE WOK

This question bothered me as we were rehearsing.

"Amber, what happened? Did someone spread a new rumor about your dad?" Brooke probed.

I stopped in the middle of Britney Spears's "Stronger." It was one of my favorites by her and really described what I was feeling. But when Brooke dipped into my past again, I nearly choked. "What did you say?"

"Sorry, I didn't mean to offend you. You just seem a little distracted. What's on your mind?" Brooke answered.

I felt my face go hot. I couldn't say that I could completely forget what happened in the past, but on the other hand, I was not up for a therapy session either. I also thought this might not be a good time to ask Brooke about her dreams. I knew that deep down inside she was also hoping to achieve something. But I couldn't lay my finger on it and I didn't feel like getting yelled at for no reason. So all I said was, "Nothing. Nothing's wrong. I'm fine."

I must not have sounded so convincing because Brooke lifted one of her eyebrows. She only did that when she was skeptical. She didn't push it though. That was incredibly nice of her. She could have tickled it right out of me like Celeste would have, knowing how ticklish I was, but she didn't.

I started over. From the top. I paused right after the first line like Britney did. I divided out certain words into two distinct syllables in the places that she did on her album. As I sang, I felt myself feeling warmer and warmer inside. The song was empowering. It felt *good*. I closed my eyes and as I finished the singing, including all the parts that echoed, I realized that I felt relaxed. Anything that made you feel that good was where you truly had to be.

Singing felt like home to me and it was where I wanted to stay.

It was nice to have the house almost empty and be able to feel just like that.

Brooke had been watching me carefully. When I opened my eyes, she seemed preoccupied with a secret memory. It was my turn to ask her what was on her mind.

"Hey Brooke. How was it? Whatchya thinking about?" I asked.

"Huh, what?"

"You look like you're daydreaming," I said.

She appeared to be having trouble deciding whether to say anything or not. Finally, she seemed to want to say it straight out. "I'm going through a quarter-life crisis, Amber."

So it wasn't just a hiatus! Well, in the back of my mind I always knew that, but ever since Revelation I had been kind of dense. Go figure.

The truth was Brooke wanted to be just Brooke, not *the* Brooke Fulton anymore.

The only problem was she realized a bit too late that being just Brooke meant being a normal teenager, which came with all the problems with being a normal teenager. She was suffering from an identity crisis. A normal teenager had to figure out what her peers were up to and either rise above the pressure to be just like everybody else or end up succumbing to the influence of others. A normal teenager had to figure out what her life goals were, which is usually what she was planning to do after high school graduation. Would she go into employment, and if so, what job should she get? Should she go to vocational school? Should she go to college, and if so, what college? What would she do with her life after that?

When you are in high school, you have to ask yourself, who am I? Of course, some just breeze through without a care in the world, imagining that high school graduation is light-years away. But most kids do give this some thought, even the ones who party a lot.

Brooke didn't really think it through. She just knew she wanted to stop being a pop star. She wanted a normal teenage girl life, complete with trips to the mall with girl friends, hanging out, sleepovers, late-night chats, Saturday nights spent with boyfriends, a life that didn't involve making music videos in front of the camera, working with adults, record producers, and publicists and the whole package that came with being a famous singer. She wanted to have time for movies and staying up all night studying for exams. She wanted to immerse herself in high school instead of having to act like a high school girl for three minutes and thirty-seven seconds in a music video. And boy, would she like not to be recognized. She wanted to wear normal teenage clothes, not a hat and sunglasses all the time. Was all this too much to ask for? Could she be given another chance to figure out who she was? If she continued down her pop-star path she may miss out on all these goodies of life forever. She wasn't sure she wanted that, even if she didn't know what exactly it was she wanted.

As I listened to her go on and on about her life and all its uncertainties, I couldn't help but wonder, is the grass always greener on the other side? I mean besides us both trying to figure out what we wanted out of life, like we figured out before, didn't we basically want to swap lives? And if we did, did that mean we were expecting the old adage to ring true? We were both at another fork in the road and while it may be hiding under a cloud of fog, we were doing our best; we were striving to climb above the fog.

I told Brooke I wanted to do a Britney

Spears cover for my demo. It seemed fitting.

"No," she said firmly. "Your demo has to be personal. It has to be you."

How quickly she turned around. Our focus had been on her life a mere second ago. She was real. You don't see many girls like that nowadays.

By the end of our session, we had decided that I had to write my own lyrics and Brooke would help me with the rest. Of course, she said she could aid me in the process of songwriting, but it had to be me. The song had to say "Amber Yang" to listeners when it was played for others to hear. They had to identify the words to me. Then, and only then, would the song be successful.

It was Thanksgiving morning!

Not everyone was as excited as I was when they woke up on that special Thursday morning that only came once a year, but I just happened to have the best attitude when it came to holidays and any excuse to stuff myself with good, mouth-watering food. Brooke said she used to have the same attitude when it came to holidays that required a big hearty appetite, but then her singing career happened. Although she had never tried to be the next live Malibu Barbie, she had never wanted to be a three-hundred-pound mass of lard either. And that tended to happen at your typical Thanksgiving when there was a twenty-four-pound golden turkey sitting on a platter, representing the centerpiece of the dining table.

Brooke groaned. That was her epic reaction to holidays as opposed to my chipper one. I laughed. It was really nice to have your best friend stay in the same house as you.

OIL IN THE WOK

This was the second time she had crashed in my room instead of the guest room she shared with her mom. She didn't get up at the crack of dawn again either. I must have been having a bad effect on her...or good, depending on how you looked at the situation. You were not supposed to groan on Thanksgiving morning.

Thanksgiving at my house was not what anyone would have imagined. We did not celebrate the holiday in the traditional way. Of course the only traditional sense I knew about celebrating Thanksgiving was the commercial kind. It was the kind you saw on TV and in the ads and wherever you looked in the shopping malls and cookbooks. We have Peking Duck instead of turkey and we tell each other the things we were grateful for during the year. And it's specific to each person. So if I was thankful for Dad helping me with a school project, then that was what I'd thank him for. We usually bought the duck from Hung Ho's around the corner the day before Thanksgiving as nearly all the stores were closed on the day. It was like a five-minute walk from our house. Dad was the one who picked it up. We ordered it about a week or so ahead of time to have it made just the way we liked it. We had to order it early because even though most people got turkey, there was a mad rush right before Thanksgiving and the big birds were usually sold out so close to the big day.

This year, even though I oddly felt the same as I did every year on Thanksgiving Day, I had no idea how it was going to go. We hadn't been one big happy family in a long while. I didn't know who was going to say what when it came time to thank each other or if things would be different now that we had Brooke and Lina with us. Would Mom require everyone to sit together at the table and then ask her old college friend plus her daughter to join us in saying our thanks?

Would Dad even be allowed to sit with us at the same table? Or would he still be in the dog house? One thing we could always guarantee at our house: it would never get boring.

There was also the problem that Brooke wasn't exactly getting along with her mom either. It didn't take me long to figure out that she wasn't happy with some of the stuff that her mom wanted her to do. One thing Lina wanted was for Brooke to get more plastic surgery done. I couldn't imagine what plastic surgery someone as beautiful as Brooke could hope to get to improve her already flawless appearance, but I could only guess that it was her mother's idea to boost her image so that she could sell more records. What a cheap scam. I wasn't even sure if you could call it that way, but as of now I was definitely seeing it from Brooke's point of view. That was a no-brainer. For as long as history stands, it will always be teens with teens, adults with adults, teens vs. adults.

No, we're not fighting a battle, but teens will understand teens better than adults can, no matter what the era. I don't make the rules. I'm just the messenger. Don't shoot me.

There had to be happy families out there. It just wasn't going to be us this Thanksgiving.

That morning I also realized that I hadn't told Brooke about our Thanksgiving tradition. Like always, I didn't know if it was my place to do it, and in the end I decided that I wouldn't say anything. Let the chips fall where they may, as they say. Of course that usually meant that I'd have to answer some questions, which would inevitably give away what I wanted to hide in the first place. Boy, was I one piece of work, let me tell you.

The house was quiet. For once, everyone was sleeping in at the same time. That was

another great thing about long weekends—
you didn't have to get up! Well, at least not on
your usual schedule. It seemed that Brooke
and I were the only ones up.

"God, I just have no idea what I'm
doing," she murmured to herself. Guess she
didn't know I was up.

"Brooke?" I asked gently. She was clearly
feeling fragile, and fragile girls didn't need
any yelling or harsh words. I should know. I'd
been through plenty of fragile times.

"Ah! You scared me!" She sat right up.

"Sorry!"

She still looked sad underneath. That was
the truth. I didn't know how a person who
made a career out of singing happy tunes and
upbeat rhymes could find herself in such a
state of mind. I mean, for someone who had
no idea where her life was taking her, she had
been hiding it very well. Until now, that is. We
sat up, her on the carpet and me on the bed,
and chatted that morning like two mature

adults. I guess I helped Brooke get part of what she wanted: the feeling of staying up late chatting with a girl friend. Even though it was morning, with the house so quiet and everyone else asleep, that's just how it felt.

Before long, Brooke's mom got up... before *my* mom. That was a first. I guess Lina had gotten used to Brooke's pop-star schedule, but now that it was the long weekend, she could finally beat a doctor's sleep schedule for once. I was just about to point this fact out to Brooke when she beat me to it. We laughed about that for a minute. Then I asked her questions about what it was like to go on tour, have screaming fans, and most importantly, how it felt to be on that stage, singing her heart out.

I was gaining ideas for my song. My demo had to be original.

We were in the middle of our chat when Lina knocked on our door. I guess my room wasn't sound proof.

Lina's red hair was amazingly in place. Her makeup was already done as well. That's just the way she was. She liked to fix herself up first thing in the morning before even letting members of her family see her. Sometimes I wondered if all her tampering with her physical appearance was the reason behind her separation from her husband. I mean, I didn't know for sure that they were separated or anything like that, but Brooke's dad was never around nor ever mentioned, so I just sort of figured...

"Good morning, ladies! Happy Thanksgiving!" It seemed, despite everything, feeling cheerful on Thanksgiving morning hadn't disappeared for Lina Fulton. In fact, she came in and gave Brooke a great big hug. From Brooke's reaction, I suspected she hadn't done that in quite a while. Two seconds later she was already dragging Brooke out of my room and apologizing for interrupting our little "gab fest." She promised to only borrow her for a few minutes before returning her to me.

There was some hidden agenda. I knew it. Maybe I was on my guard and hadn't recovered fully since that infamous night, but my intuition told me that her mom wanted something from her and it probably was going to be something she didn't want to do. What was I supposed to do in this situation? I really didn't know. With me, in situations like this I usually did nothing. Whether that was good or bad I really didn't know either; I suppose it depends on the situation.

Their arguing voices, though not very loud, woke up Mom and Dad. I knew neither one was going to admit it out of politeness, but a girl can put one and two together and get three. Every time. Aii-ya, I could tell this was going to be one happy Thanksgiving all right. I wondered if Dad even remembered to pick up the duck yesterday.

I heard the door open and Brooke's voice

suddenly getting louder, spilling across the hallway, through the walls. It sounded like she had entered the living room, with her mom right behind her. Then I heard footsteps on stairs. Mom had entered the living room as well. Oh boy. More footsteps. That would be Dad. There was only me left in my bedroom, all by myself. I didn't know if I wanted to leave it...

I ventured out slowly, careful not to knock anything over or trip. It was a bad habit of mine to be clumsy right in the middle of sticky situations when people were not agreeing and there was lots of confusion. Like now. I think Mom and Dad were just as surprised as I was at this sudden outbreak between Brooke and Lina. We had never seen either one so angry before. Apparently Brooke had been harboring these knotted emotions in her bloodstream and they had been circulating throughout her body until she was ready to burst. She didn't have the heart to disappoint her mother, but now she was having trouble keeping her feelings inside. She could speak out for anyone else, but when it came to her own troubles, she turned mute. Until now, that is. Hmmm… sounded like half of the story of my life, if such a thing existed.

The whole thing erupted before our eyes, but especially our ears, culminating in Brooke finally shouting at her mother, "I'm having an identity crisis!"

Well. That wasn't exactly what she told me, but that was close and basically said it all, whether it was for quarter-life or midlife or end-of-life or whatever time period in life, she had said it all. When you're young, you tend to think you have forever to figure out who you are; or maybe you don't even think about that deep, philosophical, sometimes existential stuff at all. When you're young, you tend to think there's always tomorrow to plan your future. You think you will live forever, that you'll be forever young. (Don't they have stores named after stuff like that? Bellemont is such a small town a lot of those big-name clothing stores never seem to make it here, which is not exactly the middle of nowhere, but it's in the same zip code.)

As soon as Brooke blurted out her big issue, the room went quiet. I didn't think that was what Brooke was going for, but it was not like we could help listening to their discord, as much as we wanted to. She turned all the way around to look at us. To her, our eyes were piercing right through her soul and seeing down to her deepest, best-kept fears and secrets. Well, at least I could imagine what it must have felt like to be her. Hasn't everyone at some point wondered if the person they have become is ultimately the person they have always wanted to be? The person they were meant to be? People at all different stages of life apply this question from many different angles. I couldn't say that I had given it a lot of thought as far as that area was concerned, but of course, I had wondered what my true calling was. They always say that you have to figure that out eventually if you want to live your life to the fullest; I had no idea if I had found my true calling, though singing came close.

In a matter of seconds Brooke had turned her personal problems into our one big extended family's problems. In order to save an awkward situation from becoming more awkward, Dad jumped in and said, "There's a way to solve this." He said it in such a way that we turned and stared at him, even Mom, because he was being so calm, and out of everyone present, we never thought he'd be the one to come in and save the day. He was the misunderstood fashion designer, shunned by his own wife, trying to figure out how to pick himself up after his fall from *Holly Doll*. I always thought that show was way too girly for him anyway. The clothes for girls that he liked to design were not quite for the girly girl and not quite for the tomboy. I didn't know how to describe it.

"They're hiring at Co~Z Monster, you know," Dad directed his remarks to Lina now. "They haven't pulled out the 'Help Wanted' sign yet, but they will starting next week. I could put in a good word and your daughter could work at the shop until she figures out what she wants to do," he suggested.

Lina looked like she was dying to interrupt, though she was kind enough not to. Nor did she make any remarks about how this was her daughter and no one else had the right to tell her how she should be raised. It just sounded like something any other parent would have said under the circumstances. Like Mom and me, she wasn't expecting him to come up with any useful ideas. I think by this time Mark Yang was used to being ignored and underappreciated, so it didn't really offend him much. We were one dysfunctional family, let me tell you.

"Th-that's not a bad idea," she finally responded. She did interrupt—she interrupted the silence.

Mark nodded his head.

"Honey?" Lina looked at her daughter with such hopeful eyes.

Brooke rolled her eyes and sighed. If Mrs. Fulton noticed, she didn't make any sign that she had. "Mo-om! How would I know? I just know that I can't go on like this anymore!"

"And how exactly is that? Taking a hiatus and then lounging around here until your celebrity status disappears and you go back to being a nobody again?"

When Brooke didn't say anything, her mother continued.

"Is that your master plan? You have always liked singing! That has always been what made you *you*! Singing has been your passion all your life and now you're just going to throw it all away?! All right, so it's understandable that it comes with some sacrifices on your body and physical appearance, but what job doesn't require you to make sacrifices? Plastic surgery comes with the business, and if you want to compete in the pop world, you've got to be a part of the pop industry," she finished. It seemed to me that once mothers were on a roll, there was no stopping them.

"Okay, Okay. Let's all sit down and discuss this rationally, together. Or we can put this to rest for today. It's Thanksgiving!" My mom chose now to chime in.

She had good intentions, I knew, but I also knew it was hard for people to put anything to rest once they had gotten themselves all worked up about it. Granted, I didn't know Mrs. Fulton as well as her daughter did, but the mother-daughter bickering session? That I knew only too well. Of course, when arguing about life decisions, that probably did not belong to the same category as the silly bickering me and Mom did. I only hoped that Lina was the kind of woman who was open to other people's good intentions.

For a second, Lina looked like she wanted to chew my mom's head off like a praying mantis. Then she gave in. "Oh, all right," she said bitterly. She looked at her daughter and added, "But I'm warning you, young lady. You better know what you want to do by the end of this break or we're packing our bags."

Brooke shrugged. Apparently reaching superstardom didn't make you immune to the wrath of overprotective mothers.

By dinnertime, the air was cleared, and even though everything was not resolved, Brooke and I still had our usual lesson. That got me real excited—working on something important to me on a holiday. That was a first. Just the fact that I even had something important to me to work on was amazing to grasp in my mind.

Towards the end, however, she asked how I would feel if I worked at Co~Z Monster with her. She told me that I didn't have to answer right away and I could figure it out over the next few days and get back to her.

Wow.

It never occurred to me that Brooke would want a friend to work with her. I always assumed that since she was fitting in really well at Serenity Creek High and Bellemont in general that she didn't worry about those kinds of things. They were more of the kinds of things I tended to worry about. It was my area, not hers. So I didn't tell her no and I didn't tell her yes. I told her I'd think about it.

It turned out that Dad still kept up with the old tradition and bought us a Peking Duck. I was real glad that while many things had changed, our Thanksgiving tradition, at least, was going to stay the same.

By the end of the break I had the first few lines of my song written. I was still working on the chorus, but at least I had it started. It was going a bit slower than I had wanted, but many projects turned out a bit differently from what was anticipated, so for once, I wasn't worried. I mean, I knew there were probably music geniuses out there who could get a songwriting project done in half the time I was going to take, maybe even a lot less than that, but I wasn't bothered by that. I am who I am, no excuses.

It was amazing that so much had happened at once. I not only had the beginnings of my song written and my parents still didn't know (no surprise there), I had a heart-to-heart talk with my mom, and Brooke and I took a chance to have a chat with my dad, together. I didn't usually seek out my father for a chat, so that was definitely a first, not just because Brooke was involved as well.

What we found was quite interesting. Mom still wanted me to consider medical school. I supposed it was her freaky "OMG!" moment where the mother realizes that her daughter's becoming a woman and will have her own life in the future without her there. She wanted me to follow in her footsteps, blah, blah, blah. She hoped I could be a doctor like her. But most important of all, she wanted me to be happy. I wasn't paying close attention when she was talking about my future career, since I heard it all before, but I was definitely touched when she mentioned my happiness. She went on to explain that when I got married, whenever that would be, I'd better find someone who cared about me. I thought that was a silly thing to say. Why would anyone marry someone who didn't care about them? Didn't that defeat the whole purpose of marriage? It was also kind of strange she should mention that, considering that at the beginning of her marriage she believed Dad really cared about her, and now things weren't going too hot. Not that he didn't care for her now, but sometimes the arguments seemed to overshadow that.

There was so much more I wanted to say

to her, but I let Mom talk. What she meant about the caring part was that the man I marry shouldn't just be smart and able to carry a decent conversation; he should truly, deeply care about me and my dreams and be okay with who I am as a person. He should want to be there for me, even if I fail or fall flat on my face. We left it at that, but it seemed that I had just gotten my first take-home lesson on love and marriage.

The chat with Dad was a little easier to take. Brooke and I were thinking about making this decision together, so it only made sense to ask Dad directly what working at Co~Z Monster was like. He was glad to fill us in. I thought that was very nice of him, all things considered. This whole broken marriage thing couldn't have been easy for him to take. Neither could this new design project he was working on, trying to enter something he wasn't sure of yet. Put those things together and I wasn't sure he'd have the energy to help us. After telling us the ins and outs of the café, he surprised me by saying a cute boy had just started working, so if we started working now, we'd have the added bonus of seeing that cute boy there.

Double wow.

Since when did my dad pay attention to that stuff? Made me wonder about his motives. I knew he wanted to help Brooke, but I wasn't sure it would apply to me, too. Maybe he wanted to keep a closer eye on me? But I wondered why he'd need to do that, considering all the visits I'd been getting from friends lately. Or maybe he really just wanted to help out, but then I felt like he was acting like a friend, not a parent. And that made me wonder, was that part of the reason Mom wanted him out?

If two people really cared about each other, how come they couldn't care enough to live together, be together, and stay together? Relationships were complicated. That was exactly why I wanted to avoid them for the time being. I just hadn't told Dad that yet. Maybe he was pretending to be interested in girl stuff to make up for the lack of time he spent getting to know me as I grew up over the years and, gee, his *huge* mistake with that woman, whoever she was…I didn't even know what had happened or if it had happened at all, but I knew that she was part of the reason why Mom wanted him to move out and, oh, get a divorce.

Ever since Revelation, I had sworn off boys…well, for the time being anyway. I knew that there was probably no way I'd ever stop crushing on some new guy, but I'd like to think that I had enough self-control not to go ga-ga over just any guy who walked my way and happened to talk to me, not that I had been getting that a lot lately. The only problem? I hadn't told anyone and now everyone seemed to be pestering me about boys. That's the way life seems to go, isn't it?

When you're interested, they aren't. When they are interested, you're not. It seemed that was the philosophy that guided every basic principle of life.

The fact of the matter was this: Brooke was seriously contemplating starting work at Co~Z Monster now that her mom had given her an ultimatum. She would feel more comfortable working there if she had me there with her. Now, if we were in middle school, I'd know that really was what she wanted. But we weren't in middle school and ever since my two ex-best friends thought they could get the best of me by not telling me the truth, I hadn't exactly been trusting too easily like I did before. It was just hard to tell if Brooke was being truthful or if she had an ulterior motive I just wasn't aware of. It seemed ridiculous because I had never questioned her intentions before, so why now?

Maybe there were just some people you knew you could trust right when you met them and there were some you knew you couldn't trust right when you met them. Nah, I was being silly. There was no such thing as that. Could you really tell by looking at people whether they were good or bad? There was no magic formula, no x-ray vision of some kind, and no way it could have been done just by looking at someone.

Maybe I trusted Brooke at first because I was in desperate need of a friend and she had never really had a best friend before. And maybe I questioned her intentions now because she was finally starting to make some new friends and they turned out to be enemies of mine. Okay, maybe *enemies* was a bit harsh, but it definitely felt that way to me. There was just a part of me that couldn't help but think that she had some hidden motive to want me to go to work with her. I couldn't think of what that would be at the moment, but was trying to avoid making the same old mistakes. I always jumped right in to something without giving it too much thought, and then when an emergency came up, or a problem I didn't think up beforehand came up, it was too late. I never looked before I leaped.

But today was a good day to start.

I started to make up a list. I wrote down every single possible thing Brooke could have in mind when asking me to join her at Co~Z Monster. I wanted to be real sure about this before I agreed to anything. This was just the safest option, and I wasn't going to take any chances. I was not about to make the same mistake twice, that was for sure—even if lots of other things weren't sure at the moment. By Sunday night I had completed my list of twenty-nine things that Brooke could have up her sleeve, and I asked her about each one directly off the list.

She practically laughed her head off. She told me she had never heard such ridiculous questions in her life. No, she was not planning on catching me off guard, taking a picture or video-taping me spilling coffee on myself and then posting it on YouTube. No, she wasn't planning on blackmailing me to my ex-best friends. No, no, and no! She thought I knew her better than that and hoped that I would never have to question our friendship again. She said she enjoyed my company and wanted to help me out with my songwriting. She figured that if I were around her more often, then during breaks and stuff she could help me with lyrics. Was she trying to bring me closer to my dad? No, that would just be an added bonus if Dad and I were to bond while at work. Actually, for me, that was another issue. Would that bring me closer to Dad or would we start getting into more fights than usual and this job would be the one thing that split us apart? It was something to consider after all. On the other hand, it might reveal some of Dad's secrets, like who he sneaks off to see. Is he really cheating on Mom or is she just being paranoid? I couldn't believe that I hadn't thought of it before! It had been months since she first started asking to get a divorce, but I had never thought of doing some of my own investigating. I mean, I always thought they were the adults and I was the kid, so what did I have to do with their personal affairs? But maybe this time would be different. Maybe this time I could dig around, get some answers, and fix their marriage! Like a marriage counselor! Suddenly this whole working at Co~Z Monster thing was looking up. Who knew that while I suspected everyone else to have a motive against me, I had my own motive all along? This was one tricky situation, but I didn't feel so bad about working at the café anymore.

And then I settled it. I needed a break from Mom, and Brooke needed a break from *her* mom, so I agreed to work at Co~Z Monster with her. It was decided. We told Dad and he said that was great. He'd get back to us Monday afternoon to confirm that there were open positions for both of us.

This was great news! I was actually excited about having an after-school job.

It occurred to me a few minutes after asking Dad to hook us up with the jobs that this was a great opportunity for Brooke to meet some new people in town and possibly make some new friends who *weren't* my worst enemies that she could hang out with. Now, of course, that would be a bonus for me as well, but I was kind of getting sick of her always tagging along with me. I realize I didn't have anyone else to hang out with either, but I was kind of hoping for some alone time. Like actual alone time where I didn't have to worry about friends for a while. I felt like that was pretty selfish of me, but I really needed time to spend with myself so I could learn about myself some more. Was that weird? Sometimes it just felt like I was the only one with these random thoughts in my head. I think I think too much. I think I analyze too much.

That was another thing about me. Lately, it seemed like every time someone started treating me well, I had the urge to push them away. Revelation had taught me to trust no one. At least that's what I thought it had taught me. It was like I was destined to be alone. It sounded selfish, preferring my own company to that of others, especially with so much going on in the world that was a lot worse than what I had experienced, but I seriously had those thoughts in my head from time to time. But I was hoping things would start to look up again once Brooke and I were working together. They already had since she began helping me out with my singing. So I was grateful for that. I should have really focused on the positives going on in my life, instead of the negatives. What was that thing that Mr. Frasca always talked about in Chemistry last year? Murphy's Law. I had to find a way to avoid that one! But it was so hard when that was exactly what I felt like I was experiencing!

Sometimes you have to step back and take a look at the big picture, but I really hated doing that. I liked being left in the dark about certain matters, just not everything. With this new job, I really didn't know what to expect. I mean, I had never really worked anywhere before, let alone make coffee drinks. Of course this was going to be a good thing. Work, get paid, buy my own stuff. I would need money if I wanted to cut a demo, right? Plus it would look good on college applications, just in case. I would learn new skills I couldn't learn in school and whatever I didn't know how to do already, someone would teach me, so that wasn't a problem for me. Ah, but there was one thing I was overlooking and it was so obvious I couldn't believe I didn't catch it right from the start. I had one other fear left: what about the customers? So many kids from our school went to Co~Z Monster, and not all came for the coffee. Many came just to hang out, and that included Karen and Serena. I mean, it had been a while, but I used to be one of those kids. At this point I mostly went to the Hoop, but that was because fewer people I knew hung out there. I hadn't even considered what would happen when I had to see my classmates all the time. I was amazed at myself for forgetting such an important part of working at Co~Z Monster. But I'd already told Dad I'd take the job, so there was not much I could do about it now. If there weren't enough new positions open, then I was off the hook, but that didn't seem very likely.

Monday rolled around and break was officially over. It was amazing how a four-day weekend could seem so long but then go by really fast. Too fast. It was always faster than you thought, and then you wondered where the time had gone. So many things you planned to do just never got done and you were already thinking about how to spend the next four-day weekend.

Well, as fast as the break went by, the school day went by so slow I thought the clock was broken. It's funny how time works. When you're doing something you genuinely enjoy, something relaxing, time passes quickly. So fast that you don't even notice it flying by. When you're doing something you don't want to do, that you don't particularly enjoy, time ticks by so slowly, second by second, and you are counting down, extremely impatient for it to pass by.

That was how it felt on Monday. I was anticipating what my dad would tell us that afternoon. I didn't know what would be coming, but either way I'd have to face it, with whatever amount of courage I could muster. I didn't know at this point if I had any courage left, but when you have to, you have to, just like the Cowardly Lion from *Wizard of Oz.*

"You guys are in!" Dad said to Brooke and me, speaking with more energy than I'd heard from him in a long time.

"That's awesome!" Brooke exclaimed, a little more enthusiastically than I had expected. I really thought working at Co~Z Monster was not high on her to-do list.

I just gave her an "are-you-serious?" look. Then I returned the low-five that she was waiting for.

When she saw my face she shot me a "what?!" look.

Dad didn't notice any of these exchanges as he continued, "You'll just need work permits from your school since you're both under eighteen, and then you'll need to go in for an interview, fill out some paperwork, and complete a one-week training process…"

As my dad went on and on about what

would be required to get set up for work, I thought about what this moment meant for me. It was my first step. It was my first big step towards making it...making a dream reality. I may fail, I thought, I may flop, and this whole thing may turn out to be one big mess, but I was making a choice, setting a decision in stone for a change, instead of hanging around, moping in the house. Because yes, it was fun to hang out in my room on Friday nights, listening to my iPod, drowning out the white noise of my parents' shouting matches, but let's face it: I couldn't go on like that forever. Things needed to change whether I liked it or not. Sometimes, when you didn't know what was right for you, you needed someone to point it out to you. In this case, it was going to be a part-time job, and Brooke.

Brooke. She was definitely making the most of her time off. Or if the time off wasn't quite time off and had evolved into time reinventing herself, she was using it wisely. Teachers at school were starting to wonder why she wasn't an official student instead of auditing the classes. The truth was she was doing so well in her classes, she'd sometimes help me with mine in her free time. That was truly remarkable. It made me wonder about her schooling background. How much schooling had she had? Did she at least finish middle school? Brooke was doing amazing. And she deserved to be with amazing people, not people like me who didn't know how to live their lives.

My mission was to get her started at work, but then she had to find some other people to hang around with. For her own good, there had to be new people more worthy of her kindness.

The rest of the week went by rather quickly, considering the slow start. Brooke and I got our drug tests done. (It was required of all prospective employees.) Then we had our in-person interviews with Dad's boss, the café manager. Of course, being high school students, when the manager asked why we wanted the job, we had to say we were gaining work experience and enjoyed helping people.

A week later, we were finally going through with training. There was a lot to learn in one week, let me tell you! I mean, in a way, it was just like what I had expected: you had to learn to operate the cash register, but you also had to learn to make the drinks. After that, you had to learn how to help clean up the shop when business was slow. At least we were getting paid. After training was done, we had to take an oral exam, a simulated on-the-job test, and a computerized test. They were very thorough and of course, we had to pass the tests. They were nice about that, though. You just had to get at least an eighty percent or higher and then, bingo! You're hired!

Oh, there was one last thing Dad had failed to mention. Since he had already been working at Co~Z Monster, he was going to oversee our work at the beginning. This was necessary before they were going to allow Brooke and me to start working on our own. Hmmm...I wasn't sure I liked this arrangement. I had hoped that if we had to go through something like that it would be with someone else, not Dad. It just seemed things would be better that way. But in life, as we all know, we don't always get what we want. Sometimes we get what we don't want.

Like on my first shift working with Brooke and Dad overseeing. Isaac was there—he was the new cute boy.

So this was the scene at good old Co~Z Monster: me, the girl who was supposed to be applying to art school with at least one parent who wanted her to go to medical school and had no idea this daughter was hiding attempts at writing her own song to become a pop singer; Sally Hunter, who was really Brooke Fulton, pop-star diva in hiding, going through her quarter-life crisis; Dad, the cheating soon-to-be-ex-husband and failed fashion designer who was trying to re-create his dream of becoming the next big thing; and Isaac, the senior from my health class who had no idea who these people were. Did anyone know who these people were?

Usually when a schoolgirl has a crush on a boy from school, she becomes nervous and speechless. Well, I can assure you that Amber Yang did *not* have a crush on Isaac, contrary to what Brooke thought, but I still had no idea what to say to him. Should I avoid talking about anything that had to do with school and just stick with work-related topics, or was it okay to talk to him about health class and school and everything else that required an actual conversation and not just a yes or no kind of thing?

The question was this: if I truly didn't have a crush on him, why was I showing all the signs that I did? Did that mean I subconsciously liked him or something and just didn't want to come out and admit it? There was a lot of iffiness here, but I couldn't explain any of it yet. I just had to go with the flow. Of course, I wasn't happy that it turned out the boy Dad had mentioned was someone I knew from school. It was not like he could help it or anything, it wasn't his fault, but it was just...I never expected it. (That seemed to be happening a lot lately, didn't it?)

Aaargh. I had to come to terms with the fact that maybe I just had a hard time dealing with stuff that happened out of nowhere. It seemed ridiculous, like everyone else was so good at handling stuff and then there was me, a completely hopeless wreck of a case.

And what did Isaac have to do with my hopes, my fears, and my dreams? Was I going to sing a song about him some day? Of all the people in the world who could have started working at the same place as me, why was it him? I didn't really believe in destiny, but at times like these the thought did creep into my brain. Plus, the added fact that I started working there almost right after he started must have looked creepy and stalkerish from his angle, I was sure. He had to be thinking that I was just that crazy girl from his group that random day in class who all of a sudden wanted to be a groupie so I picked up a shift where he worked just to get close to him. I mean, there was a possibility that he saw all this as just a coincidence, but I highly doubted that. I didn't know much about guys, but it seemed to me many teenage boys had huge egos. Of course, that may have been something pop culture had influenced my thinking with and I could have been very wrong, but boys just seemed to assume you were stalking them when in reality it was just a coincidence that you happened to be working at the same place at the same time.

None of this analyzing could actually

help me get through the working part or help me decide why I cared about the opinion of a boy whom I wasn't even sure I liked, or why I even cared about his opinion in the first place. In fact, it only confused me more about what I wanted for myself, and having to wonder how I acted around him made me ask, who am I really? Because didn't it go back to how I acted in front of everyone that ultimately decided who I was as a person?

There was a lot running through my mind. Every moment wasn't just a moment that passed by anymore. Every moment was another chance to grow, to change. Every moment was defining, helping me see myself for who I really was. I just hoped that each moment was bringing me one step closer in the right direction. Of course, I wondered about this all the time, but part of me knew the answer to all this muddle: I was afraid of Isaac finding out about Dad's situation.

Dad didn't know that I saw Isaac in school every day. Dad didn't know that Isaac was a senior at Serenity Creek High and not some random cute boy I was interested in. He didn't know I had sworn off boys for the time being. And no, that did not mean I was into girls now. Har, har. It just meant that my life was confusing enough as it was without the added complication that crushes brought. So I wanted to un-complicate things by eliminating that part of my life altogether for a while. See, I was being practical. I didn't know who I was just then, and to be with someone, I had to know who I was first. Because how could I have a boyfriend if I didn't even know what kind of person I was? As my mom always said: Career first, then boyfriend. I didn't know much about my future, but that much I did know. That was the direction I wanted to go, and I hoped my defining moments would push me down that path.

Then again, maybe Mom had it wrong. Perhaps Mom spent so much time pushing herself down that path that by the time she was ready for a boyfriend, she found herself with the upper hand when it came to being independent. The men she met couldn't match her independence, so she settled for the next best thing—a man with passion for what he did. The only problem was, she found out too late that just having passion didn't lead to a successful career. Sure, Mark loved fashion with a passion, but he lacked some necessary qualities to make it big. Something was simply missing from him. Iris had already waited years for it to bloom, to no avail. This is going to sound harsh, but I didn't want to end up like Mom. An even harsher want? I didn't want to end up like Dad either.

At the coffee shop we were allowed to have free drinks if orders got messed up and discounted drinks, bagels, cookies, and basically anything else we wanted just for being an employee. Those were just some of the perks of working at Co~Z Monster. Of course, there was also the fact that I got to spend time working on the demo with Brooke outside of class and home, which was always a good thing, considering it meant there was less of a chance of anyone walking in on us. Though, of course, we had to be careful since Dad had to work the same shifts at the beginning. Luckily, after we were done with our on-the-job training and took off our training wheels, so to speak, we were able to have different shifts from Dad. That was fine by me and Brooke. We didn't mind working the same shifts as Isaac, though, even when we were working on the demo. What was he going to do? It wasn't like he would have any say and we weren't friends with him or anything. It was less awkward with him around than when my dad was there. Is that weird?

I guess working with family could go both ways. You could either get along real well at the workplace and be real comfortable with each other or you could get sick of each other. I mean, people get tired of seeing each other all the time, and, when they're together at work and at home, they have no option but to fight. It's just like when both spouses feel that they should be the one in control. When both sides cannot come to an agreement about something, a lot of arguing will ensue as a result. That was why I was glad that Dad wasn't always around.

Balancing school with work turned out to be amazingly straightforward and easy. I had to admit that at first I was worried, but then I realized that there were days when business was slow, so I could always bring my Biology textbook with me and lay it on the counter to read during my downtime. I didn't get all of my homework done, mostly AP Bio, but that helped a lot because when I got home, tired, at least I knew that I didn't have all my homework left to do, just the rest of it. It was a great feeling—something I didn't want to let go of, but I knew that like all good things, it would eventually come to an end.

In her downtime, Brooke, whose name tag read Sally, would bust out some napkins and a pen and scribble a few words here and there with what I could only assume were for the lyrics to my demo. Homework was optional for her and she wanted to spend free time helping me out with my songwriting. That was so generous of her and it only made me feel worse about my secret motive. Why was I always so soon to push people out of my life when they were banging on the door?

OIL IN THE WOK

Was it because I was jealous of Brooke's incredible focus? I mean, she may have been a lot like me, unclear of the road ahead and of who she was outside of the pop-star world, but she could work on any project any time anywhere without worrying about the same things that I worried about all the time. She didn't think about who was watching or who she ran into during the day or who she had to work with. She just did it. Like Nike. Maybe secretly I wanted to have the same kind of spirit that she had. Maybe I wanted to be that focused. I certainly didn't want to be my self-conscious schoolgirl self forever and ever, without changing. Because what I was, it seemed to me, was stuck at the fork in the road and not knowing which way to turn. I was afraid to take a step in either direction. What if no matter what I chose, I failed? But most importantly, why was it so hard for me to believe in myself, but so easy for Brooke to believe in me? I only saw the bad in me, the faults, but she could see the good, the strengths. It didn't make sense. I always thought that a confident person would just exude this air of sureness about himself or herself, no questions asked. Confidence was something a person had and it couldn't be seen, visually. It just existed and it wasn't something you had to work out. Cheerleaders, athletes, celebrities, they all just *had* it. It wasn't something they were born with, but one day they just had confidence. It was like the fairy dust of self-esteem burst over their heads and it was sprinkled over them one night before they went to bed and when they woke up the next morning, they were confident and that was that.

I know, I know. That wasn't true at all. It was only in my mind, but for some reason, I couldn't stop seeing it that way. After all, what had I got to lose with a friendship with Brooke? The truth of the matter was, she was my only friend right now and only

172

because she happened to be a client of my mother's. For once in a long time, I had someone to do stuff with and I didn't sing by myself listening to my iPod on Friday nights. I didn't mind being by myself, but as much as I enjoyed alone time, I couldn't help but admit that it could get, well, lonely. Was that all I needed? Company? A best friend to hang out with again? Was I angry with Karen and Serena for taking that away from me in one night? Or was I angry with myself for not being able to pick myself up from this blow, for letting myself be affected in the first place? Was that it? Was I angry because I couldn't show the real me in front of everyone and I had to stay quiet and pretend that art was my thing and that's all I ever cared about? But there was a reason for that, wasn't there? I couldn't tell everyone that I wanted to be a singer because I could fail, and then where would I be?

Maybe I was just being stubborn

because everyone always says that "you only fail when you don't try" and although it sounded cheesy and all, I was starting to think that they may be right. I had heard it a thousand times or more and it was like one of those sayings that people say when you're feeling like a failure. It's what they say when they don't know what else to say to make you feel better. But the thing is, sometimes you want something so bad you absolutely refuse to fail. If you fail, that will be the end of you. Just trying is not enough. You *have* to reach that goal.

It was a Wednesday afternoon, after the mad rush when school just let out. I always wondered why so many people enjoyed having coffee right after school, but I never really figured it out. Did they find it stress-relieving after a long day? Did they need to stay awake during the afternoon? If they did, what for? The hardcore homework kids, as far as I knew, worked on homework late into the night. They were practically nocturnal. If anybody needed coffee to stay awake, that would be the time to drink it, not in the afternoon. I didn't know, considering I was not one of those hardcore homework kids myself, I wouldn't know. Brooke kept messing up her orders, even though there weren't that many. In fact, she and I were the only ones behind the counter now that the school kids had cleared out. Something was occupying her mind, and I wanted to help her before she started spilling espresso all over the place. She had messed up so many orders we had enough free drinks to last us through the rest of the week and practically all of next week as well. Something was definitely up. It was really unlike Brooke.

When people seem preoccupied, there are five things to consider before you can decide if you should help them, talk to them, or just leave them alone. Number 1: What's their facial expression? Are they troubled, angry, worried, sad? Does their face say it's okay to walk over and start shooting the breeze? Number 2: What are they working on? Are they holding a knife to chop vegetables? Is there room on the couch to sit down next to them in case they want to talk? Number 3: Is this a good time? Will they be gone for a month on a road trip with friends before they get a chance to respond? Timing is so important, but people always seem to be off with it. It's the first thing that is messed up in many situations. Number 4: What are you going to say to them? Could you offer any advice or say something that would potentially improve their frustrations, or would you exacerbate their situation? Do you have anything positive to say? Number 5: Do you have the time to comfort them? People have problems and issues to deal with on a regular basis and so do you. If you offer someone a shoulder to lean on and then they end up taking up too much of your time, would you feel used or like you just wasted a lot of your precious time? Would you feel bad when the comforting is over and you have less time to finish what you were working on?

When I saw Brooke struggling to keep the orders straight, I forgot these five things and walked right over, deciding to ask her what was up. She had been so good to me these past few weeks that I figured it would be rude not to show any bit of concern for her well-being. This girl had a lot more going on than just a hiatus from her career. She needed help, whether she realized it or not. We were not in the same situation, but we were both girls, and as girls, we had to stick together. In the end, through it all, good friendships and friendships that tear us down, we had to stick together.

Of course, I opened with the absolute best line possible: "Are you all right?"

Brooke looked tired, but not angry like

she was going to lash out at me for asking or anything, so that was good. Looked like today I didn't need my list. That was a relief. She nodded her head while keeping it down and answered, "Yeah, I'm fine."

I was about to respond, but then she added with a slight smile, "Thanks for asking."

Now I know usually when you go to offer someone comfort, they are the one who is supposed to feel better. But for some reason, when she added that at the end, I felt better. It was weird. I think I felt more comforted than she did and I know that was not supposed to happen. I didn't really have anything to feel better about either. No, that couldn't be right. I had to ask, to probe, to get to the bottom of this. I wasn't really helping her by letting the subject drop. Of course, at the same time, I didn't want her to feel cornered. That couldn't result in anything good. I decided to step back and wait. It was nearly time for me to take over the orders and her to work the register. That would give her a break from making drinks.

I really admired her. She was being so strong, holding up even when she obviously couldn't wait until her shift was over. I knew the feeling well. Sometimes you just wanted to get through with something. You were not really caring if you did it well; you just wanted to get it over with so that you could go back to trying to handle your problems or whatever was on your mind. Just finishing whatever you had to finish would free you up to face what you needed to face.

It was time to switch. I logged off my account on the register and brought the screen back to the sign-on menu. I hoped that she would remember to type in "Sally Hunter" and not "Brooke Fulton." On the first day of work, she almost typed her real name before stopping and realizing the blunder she was about to make. The manager looked puzzled and Dad just pretended not to have noticed.

Brooke seemed to know that it was time to switch, but when she walked over to sign herself in, she started typing "Broo" before catching her mistake and typing "Sal" instead. She was distracted, but while most people our age would have probably hit the machine or cursed or uttered some obscenity, she didn't.

"Are you sure you don't want to talk about it?" I asked.

Brooke looked up at me. "We'll talk at home, okay?"

I nodded, hoping that she really meant what she said. Some people always say, "Let's talk about this later," but you know in the back of your mind that they are only saying that to avoid talking about it at all, and when it is really "later," they pretend not to remember. If Sally did that, this wasn't going to be good. This time, something huge, maybe life-altering had happened and it wasn't the way she had imagined it to be, so she didn't really want to talk about it. That was understandable, but now that only made me more curious about what had been going on. I suspected it had something to do with her mom, but I couldn't quite lay my finger on it yet. We spent the last forty-five minutes of our shift in silence, just responding to customers and the occasional head nod. That was it. It was uneventful and quiet.

It turned out I didn't have to wait that long to hear about Brooke's problems. As we were driving home (my car, Brooke riding shotgun), she started talking. Some of the things she said, I already knew from the Thanksgiving break discord. She was still confused about what she was supposed to be doing with her life, and she wasn't sure what was next. But then she laid down the bare facts, the part she'd been afraid of, and the part she'd been frustrated with.

"I think I'm good at this, you know?"

she said. "Even before singing, I think I've always been good at school."

Of all the things I thought she was going to tell me, I didn't think Sally Hunter of all people would be the one to be giving me a lesson about how to stay in school. I let her continue though. It was rude to interrupt someone with your own problems when you promised to be the listener.

"I really like Biology. I mean, I'm good at it. And I like it. I haven't enjoyed doing something since I became serious with my singing. I feel like all I'm doing is selling records. I want to go to a regular high school where no one recognizes me, study, go to college as a Biology major and then onto medical school. Because I am good at it!"

She paused for breath, punctuating her last thought, before going on.

"I want to be a doctor. I know there's something out there for me, not about singing, that I could spend the rest of my life doing, something I would love to do and actually enjoy, and I think that's being a doctor. I mean, singing is great, but I don't think that's my true calling. My true calling has got to be Biology. Even if I don't end up in medical school or whatever, I've gotta be studying Biology! I've gotta be using a microscope and making observations about an amoeba. That is my true calling!" She got all worked up and started breathing heavily for a few seconds. I still didn't say anything. We were almost home by now.

"And this...this working at a coffee shop while waiting for life to happen...this isn't me," she continued. "This isn't what I'm meant to be doing! I need to be out there, in the gardens, in the yard, at the zoo, experiencing what it's like to...to...to live. To be. To exist in the wild..."

I pulled into the driveway.

"Like have you ever watched a bird? Like really watched a bird? They stick their little

YUMIN YE

beaks into the ground and—bam!—there's a worm. How do they do that? That's what I want to know. I want to conduct experiments to see how the wind blows. I want to know how a monarch butterfly knows which way to fly when it migrates. Don't you get it? Doesn't anyone get it?"

With this sudden outburst, while we were standing in the front yard, I had to interject, "Whoa, what happened? Am I missing something? What's holding you back?"

"Lina," was all she offered. She was staring at her feet, at a blade of grass. That was very unlike the Brooke Fulton I knew. That was her punctuation.

This just amazed me. I had a feeling that her problems had something to do with that woman, but when all she did was offer that name like that, just one word, I couldn't help but wonder, did we always blame our problems on the parental units? Is that what teenagers did? Did we just make that

184

up as an excuse for why we weren't where we were supposed to be? She was probably going to tell me why Lina was the one holding her back, but I was just stunned when she uttered her mother's name like that. Everything could seriously be summed up by one person's name? It might have been that easy for Brooke, but it wasn't that simple for me.

She wasn't done, however.

"I can't get her out of my head, you know?"

I nodded my head in agreement even though I didn't understand. I'd like to think that maybe yes, Mom could get on my nerves sometimes and bug me about stuff, but she never stood in the way of my dreams. Granted that I was hiding my singing project, but that was different. I was just hiding from failure and embarrassment because I had already changed my life goals more than once. Yet, whenever I'd been truthful with her, Mom had always been supportive and encouraging.

"She's always telling me what I'm doing wrong. Ever since I was little. God, sometimes I really wonder if singing was my idea or hers!"

I was getting seriously confused now… didn't all mothers do that?

"It's like she heard me singing one day, and yes, maybe I had the talent. Yes, maybe it was fun at first. But I really didn't wake up one morning and say, 'I think I'll be a pop star now.' You know? I mean, come on! I was, what, four, five? I sang 'Simple Gifts' and all of a sudden my mom thinks I'm hitting every note on key and the next thing I know she's making me practice and rehearse, rehearse, rehearse so that I could get noticed, God! And yes, I got better, I learned how to expand my vocal range and for a while, this seemed like the good path to take, but now…now it's different. I don't want to be coaxed into singing, into marketing myself to the public so that I can sell records. I want a do-over! I want to have my own opinion on what I want for my life, not some commercialized formula for success. What is that? *Lina*, yes, that's what I'm calling her now, all she has done since then is tell me what I have to change about myself to make it even further in this business. This business? Excuse me? Since when is my life all about how to make it in this business? The music industry? When did my life become all about selling stuff? What exactly am I selling anyway? Pop music? Or an image that speaks to young girls and makes them think that as long as they are nice, pretty, and fit they'll find their Prince Charming one day and live happily ever after? Is that the message we are spreading to the young girls of today?"

Brooke had just said a mouthful. I wasn't sure I had exactly followed her either. How did her argument pertain to her relationship with

Lina, for example? Or was she simply angry at the world for making her who she was?

"All right, time to go inside," Brooke said calmly. She spoke so much softer than she had a second ago I was afraid. This was definitely an outburst of emotion that she had been hiding all along. She must have been planning to discuss it with someone at some point, but apparently she never got around to it 'til, well, right *now*.

After that huge tirade, all I could do was follow her inside. What else could I do? You never wanted to talk back or respond right away after someone just spilled like that. If you did, you ran the risk of the person lashing back at you, because in that moment, no matter who was right and who was wrong, you would always be wrong, and the angry one would always be right. So the best thing to do was to wait for some time to pass before putting in your two cents…or five…

Thankfully when we walked inside, the

infamous Lina wasn't there. I didn't know what would have happened if she had been there, but I was definitely glad she wasn't. No one was home, actually, but I knew that, being almost 6:00 p.m., there were bound to be parents walking through the door any moment now. I just hoped we could escape into the quiet of my room so Brooke and I could fix whatever was going on in her mind. However convoluted her thoughts had become, we were going to find the best way to extricate herself from such complications. I knew I was just another girl, but sometimes if we just looked through the lens of another pair of girl's eyes, we would find what we were looking for.

Ever since our moms had found out that Brooke was sleeping in my room more often than she was sleeping in the guest room with Lina, they decided she could move in with me. My room was smaller than the guest room, but we liked this arrangement better for sure. It was like an all-girls slumber party every night. Not that there was an actual party—we were only two girls, after all.

Brooke really liked school. I knew why. I couldn't believe I didn't see it before! I mean, she really was good at Biology and basically every school subject she'd been auditing. She had the drive, the passion, and the love for it, and this was what she excelled at. She was the only one I knew who could finish the homework assignments both quickly and correctly. She was born to do this work. Why did she ever quit school? If she loved it that much, how did she ever let someone else, even her mom, decide for her, dictate, what her life was going to be all about? Did we all trust our mothers so blindly that we forgot who we were and what we enjoyed the most? Did we lose ourselves in the process of doing what our parents told us to do? Was that the real problem?

Suddenly I was seeing things in a new

light—in Brooke's light, albeit refracted.

She was still ranting when we reached my room. "I want to do this. I want to quit singing in front of twenty thousand fans, I want to stop worrying every two seconds how my face and my hair looks, I don't want to get any more plastic surgery done; God, is there really a need for rhinoplasty? I mean, seriously, do I have to hate myself just because my body isn't perfect? I want to be normal for a change. Just *normal*. Is that too much to ask? A normal girl with normal dreams. That's *it*. No more, no less. I am capable of taking care of myself!"

It looked like she had reached the end of her speech. She was looking me dead in the eye. Was I Lina? Was she practicing what she wanted to say to Lina on me? I didn't say anything at first, expecting her to go on with her outburst, but then, we heard the front door open. There were voices. They belonged to Mom and Lina.

Brooke furrowed her brows. She stared at the door to our bedroom. I knew what she was thinking. I didn't know what to say yet, but I also didn't want her to act on what she was thinking. I had a matter of seconds to act before she did what she wanted to do.

But before I could say or do anything, it was too late.

Brooke zipped out the door like a cheetah and started verbally attacking her mom. I didn't run after her, but I heard it all. Then, two seconds later, I heard the front door open and shut again and a car starting up in the driveway. I ran to my window and I saw Brooke driving away in her car, with Lina shouting after her, also in the driveway, watching her only daughter escape the house that was supposed to be her safe haven, but had turned her life into such a tangled web.

Somehow, I had the feeling that what we had just seen of Brooke was her reverting back to the old days before her superstar training. I was convinced that the pop-star persona was not the real her, and seeing things from Mrs. Fulton's side, the situation seemed to get a bit out of control when Brooke lost her temper. I could only imagine what it was like when she had a full-on touring schedule. Although Lina probably made it hard for her daughter, her daughter couldn't have made her mother's life easy either. I wanted to take Brooke's side, but what with her gone and all, plus this new realization, it was hard to. I didn't like taking sides. It was definitely not top on my list of favorites.

However, we now had a missing girl on our hands and there was nothing to indicate where a girl with a broken heart would go when left to her own devices. This is the part where the questions come and I have one of two choices to act on: I could either cooperate and tell my interrogators exactly what I do and don't know, or I could make up random answers to lead them off the trail. Was Brooke ready for some tough love or was it better to just let this thing thaw out? Once again, I had a matter of seconds to decide what to do, and unless I pulled some fast escape of my own, it looked like I was going to have to figure this one out right now.

"Amber!" Mom was coming up the stairs.

"Yes, Mom!" I answered.

Her face was appearing at the door. "Brooke just left. Do you have any idea where she might be headed?" Mom was a bit out of breath. Looked like she had run up the stairs. This was serious indeed.

After much deliberation, I answered the truth. "Nope."

"Come on, Amber, you've got to know something! This is no time to mess around!"

"Co~Z Monster?" I knew that I wasn't

really helping, but I wasn't doing any damage either, was I?

Mom was starting to look angry. But before she could say or do anything, the front door burst open, yet again. Lina barged into the house, shouting, "I'm calling 9-1-1!"

Now both Mom and I found ourselves running down the stairs.

This! Wasn't! Happening! Sure, Brooke had run away, but did it really need to be reported to the authorities? I had a feeling we were going to be too late…

By the time we had finally gotten ourselves into the living room where the nearest landline was located, Lina was already holding the phone to her ear. She wasn't even watching us. Mom ran over to the cradle and hung up the phone by pushing the dial tone button. It seemed that she had gotten there just in time—right before 9-1-1 did. She was super fast.

"What are you doing?!" Lina was clearly

not happy with Mom's decision. "Release that button now!" Lina commanded, but Mom didn't comply. I couldn't believe what my eyes were witnessing. My whole life, I had never imagined that one day I'd have to watch my own mother fight with someone else's mother about anything. Sure, she was currently in a legal dispute with Dad, but this? This was totally unexpected! I mean, yes, Brooke was technically missing, and as her mother, Lina was really freaking out. I realized, even though I was not a mother and probably wouldn't be for several years, that a missing child worries parents to death. However, Lina had better calm down. There had to be a better way to solve this problem than getting the police involved. Brooke didn't exactly "run away" or anything. She had simply taken her car for a drive. Plus she had only been gone ten minutes. I was sure she'd be back in time for dinner; I mean, she wouldn't be late for that, right?

Of course, she did have a part-time job now, so technically, she could go grab dinner elsewhere...

Now, I didn't know about Lina, but I was sure some of these same thoughts were running through Mom's head as well. We tended to read each other's minds a lot because of this. I guess what they say is true—great minds think alike. I had a feeling that if Brooke were here, she would have come up with five different ways to experiment, complete with a hypothesis and everything. Then she'd probably write up a lab report with materials and methods and the procedure thingy. Gosh, if I had a scientific brain like hers, I'd probably be wanting to do the same things that she did.

Mom and Lina may have been best friends in college, but of the two women, Mom was definitely the sensible one. Not that there was anything wrong with being rash. Sometimes it's good to be rash. You don't want to always be so indecisive you can't pick a flavor of ice cream when the ice cream man asks you what you want. You'd hold up the line and no one likes a line-holder-upper. But when it comes to reporting something to the police or leaving it as is, rash is not a good quality to have.

Luckily, being the sensible one comes with its benefits. You get to calm everyone down so heads can clear and people can make the best possible decision for their lives. Mom persuaded Lina to hand her the phone. She put it back in the cradle. Hopefully we wouldn't be making any more 9-1-1 distress calls. However, this simple placement of the phone back to where it belonged prompted Lina's sobbing.

Lina fell, crumpled to the floor. She was like a helpless baby, crying out for her mama to return. I didn't know whether to feel sorry for her because she never looked so pathetic, or if I should feel touched that beneath that tough skin there was a heart.

Mom tried to get her to shush, reassuring her that her daughter was going to come back sooner or later and there would be nothing to worry about. She also promised that if Brooke didn't come back in a couple of hours, she'd call 9-1-1 herself. That only seemed to make Lina sob harder. I wondered if Lina knew she had been too tough on her daughter and was blaming herself. Why did we do that? When something bad happened to someone we knew or someone we really cared about, why did we automatically blame ourselves? Did this guilt trip we put ourselves on really make us feel better? Or was it only a way to mask the pain of loss?

In the meantime, Mom slipped into the kitchen and got started on dinner. Just then, Dad marched through the front door. For once, he looked happy. I could almost detect a flicker of a smile on his face. He had a secret. He wasn't telling yet, but considering he and I were still on good talking terms, I figured it wouldn't be so hard to fish it out of him soon. I just had to wait for the right time. Lately, Dad had been good with not telling. He had news, but he would keep the news to himself until he felt like it was safe to reveal it. He knew that timing was everything.

Dad saw Lina on the floor and the smile disappeared. The look on his face said that he was debating whether to reach out or not. Lina was Mom's friend, not his, so he wasn't bound to help her; plus he and Mom were supposed to be getting separated. Well, divorced actually. On the other hand, Dad had always been sympathetic to women, especially those who were crying all alone on the floor. I guess that was his tragic flaw or weakness or whatever. It was really funny though. Mom was never the crying type of woman. He married a tough one, one who could get herself through anything. She was different from the type he usually fell for, so he chose her over all the crying women he had met. The only problem was she became a bit too controlling. She was too confident, and too un-crying, shall we say, for lack of a better word. Unshakeable. Mom had always known what she wanted, exactly how to get it, and how to avoid the distractions that would take her away from achieving her goals. She'd rather bleed to death than let tears fall helplessly from her eyes into the palms of her hands. She was the strongest person I knew. She may have been hard on me, but she also believed in me and I knew that she could fix pretty much anything and conquer whatever got in her way.

Mom believed in Dad, once upon a time. That was why they married in the first place. But I guess he had failed one too many times or something because one day, she stopped believing. There was a part of me that knew it was not quite that simple. There was something else that Mom found out about Dad that stopped her from believing in him. But amidst all the rumors that had been flying around, I had no idea what the truth was anymore. They say that the truth will set you free, but at that moment, I didn't know if that was true. Did I even want to know the truth? It seemed like the truth would be a trap, rather than something that would set me free.

"Brooke's gone," I said to Dad, before he could ask any questions. I didn't want to say "she ran away" because I was afraid of what Lina's reaction would be if I did. It would have seemed final, too real, and she would have been deeply hurt.

He looked from Lina to me. Then back again. Lina didn't even seem to notice Dad standing there. Neither did Mom, who couldn't hear anything above the sounds of her stir-frying with oil in the wok. The tension inside the house was getting just as hot as the oil. I guessed it was just me and my dad. That was rare, considering he usually didn't make his presence known, except for the sound of his sewing machine.

We all knew he was working on a new project, but there was no way to know what it was exactly, since he didn't really discuss those things. Mom had stopped believing in him, but she also hated his keeping things a secret. She still liked to know what he was working on, so long as he was staying at the house. I thought this was where they differed in opinion—he was thinking that as long as she was not on his side anymore, why should he have to check in with her? He was not about to share everything with her, opening himself up to ridicule when his new plan failed again. I thought Mom was being generous letting him stay and get by without telling her what he was up to. It was a personal project for Dad. It always was. He didn't want to reveal it until he knew he was going to receive some amount of success because of it. I knew that feeling well. It was like me and my singing project. I wanted to work on cutting a demo, but I had no idea how good it was going to be or if it was going to be worth anything at all. If I was going to say anything to anyone, I wanted my demo to already be sent out and getting some positive feedback. But if the demo wasn't even ready, I didn't want to say anything about it, for fear that once I did, it wasn't going to amount to anything. That was what Dad was doing. If he told Mom what he was working on, she'd just scoff and write it off as another one of his failed projects.

"She'll be back. She'll be fine," was all Dad offered before heading downstairs.

Wow. That was brutal. Today was not a day for him to be sympathetic to women and their troubles. His project must have been going well. More than well. I really wanted to ask him, but I held myself back. Things like this required patience.

Mom had finished making dinner. Lina had finally stopped crying. Brooke, however, was still not home. No one had called 9-1-1. It seemed that Mom believed in Brooke, even if she didn't believe in her own husband anymore. She was still banking on the fact that no matter how late it was, Brooke was still going to make it home in time for dinner. She was wrong. Brooke never made it home for dinner, not that it was much of a dinner. Dad didn't eat with us; Lina barely touched anything and decided to go to bed and deal with everything the next day. I was grateful she had stopped sobbing at least. One person could only cry so much before the energy to be sad was all used up. Yes, it takes a lot of energy to be sad.

I ate everything on my plate, but I was still thinking about Brooke. What was she doing now? Was she feeling bad for leaving us in the dark? Was she on her way back? I understood that she needed some time to herself to think things through. But it just seemed she could have accomplished that without taking off like that. What did she think she was accomplishing by rushing off? Would I have done the same in her position? I didn't know. But I knew she was very frustrated with herself. Is that what people did when they got frustrated? Find a temporary escape from their problem?

The phone! It was ringing! It was the first time the phone had rung all evening. I ran to pick it up.

"Amber," the voice on the other line said. It was Brooke! It was funny how sometimes just as you were thinking about someone, the phone would ring and you would hear her voice right then and there. I mean, it was not like telepathy existed, but I guess this predicting the caller thing came close.

"HEY!" I couldn't help it.

"Shh! Not so loud! I just called to let you know that I'm staying over at a friend's and I'll be back tomorrow. I'm fine."

Dial tone.

Wow, that was real nice of her. Remind me to get her a Christmas present.

Well, at least I knew she was all right and she would be all right for the night, and I would see her soon enough. When the phone went off, Mom came running again and I told her what I had found out. Surprisingly, the ringing hadn't woken Lina up, so we decided to let her sleep. Mom would tell her in the morning. That was the best way to go. Mom, though tough in many situations, looked so relieved to hear the news. I was glad. I hated to see Mom sad or distraught. Now I couldn't wait until tomorrow. Brooke was going to have news to tell me! It was going to be exciting, I sensed, even though I had no idea what she was going to say to me when she got home. The biggest question on my mind, though, was who was this friend she was staying with? I mean, I knew she knew other people besides me, but who else was she close enough to that they'd let her crash there for the night? Was she even going to be in school tomorrow?

Then, one person popped into my head. Of course! That was the only other person we both knew, well, besides the unnamable ones. You know what? Karen and Serena from now on shall be referred to as the Untouchables. Last year in English we read Siddhartha, and even though this had nothing to do with the book, I wanted to call them the Untouchables because that was what they were to me. Now I had two facts I was hoping to confirm; I just had to wait until the next day to find out if I was right. The only thing was, if it turned out that I was right about who this new friend was, I wouldn't know how to feel. It had to be someone else. How could it be him?

It seemed like it would take forever to get to Thursday, but here we were. Wednesday was finally over. The clock had spoken. The verdict would soon be disclosed. We would know whether Brooke had been truthful and what she had been up to. Was it lame that my life had devolved into figuring out what was going on with part pop star, part normal girl Brooke Fulton? I mean, in a way, I was living every teenybopper's dream, but in another way, I was also living every teenage girl's nightmare. If Brooke went missing forever, we'd make headline news and it would be even more attention I'd been getting on account of Mom's job.

I had a lot to be nervous about that day.

When I got to school, even the air seemed a bit more subdued than before, as if all the kids in the hallways knew what had happened already and were buzzing about it to each other in between classes in quiet, hushed tones. It could have been just my imagination, but it seemed that everyone was staring at me a little more than usual. I mean, there was no standard amount or anything, but I guess it was just that paranoid feeling, you know? I wasn't even sure what I had to be afraid of exactly because it was not like I did anything wrong or something. It was like I was afraid that Sally was going to be missing from school and then everyone was going to think I had something to do with her disappearance. But that couldn't be it because she just had to get back today. She just had to.

By the time I made it to health class, I

didn't know why, but I didn't feel too good. I knew something was wrong. My intuition was telling me so.

And it was right.

Isaac was absent. So was Brooke.

At first I thought she was just going to slip in late this morning, but when she never showed up, my heart sank. Noticing Isaac's empty seat made my heart sink even lower. Whatever Brooke had been up to, she had dragged my I-don't-know-if-I-like-him crush in with her, too. That was just wrong. I wasn't jealous. I was surprised that she thought she knew him well enough that she could ask him this favor of letting her crash. But then again, he was a senior—he probably thought girls would be falling all over his feet. I knew it was mean of me to assume such things, but it was easier than facing the real possibility that maybe he and Brooke were friends. I wondered if he'd figured out who Sally Hunter really was by now or not. I was going to take a wild guess and say no. Brooke wouldn't just tell him, would she? She worked so hard to keep her real identity concealed that if she just went and told him, what would that mean? As far as I knew, no one else had figured out who she was besides me and my family. If she told him, then that would violate her privacy, compromising everything we had worked hard to protect. And Isaac looked to be one of the trustworthy ones. Who even knew what would happen if she ended up staying over at someone else's? Anyone else and it would have been all over school that she wasn't really Sally Hunter. Who's to say that Isaac wouldn't tell?

All of a sudden I didn't understand Brooke at all. Did she really want to live the rest of her life in hiding like this? Could that even be considered a life? There was so much I wanted to ask her and so much I wanted to tell her at the same time, but it really wasn't my place to do that. At that moment I just wanted an explanation from her. After all, with her missing one night like that, we never got around to my daily lesson like she had promised. My song was just about finished, but it still needed a lot of tweaking. It desperately needed the help and attention of a professional. Some things required the ears of a real singer who understood her craft better than I did. Only that person could help me fix it and Brooke was that person for me. Where would I go without her? I was the luckiest girl alive to have the help of a real live pop star. So why did it feel like my world would be crashing down soon? Or was I simply being too dramatic?

Answers to questions never came easily. They always appeared at the strangest moments, when you were least expecting clarity. When you hit that moment of clarity, it was like—bam!—right on your forehead. It could knock you out like a piano falling from the sky, and you wouldn't even know what hit you until it was too late. I was hoping that I would get some answers before that happened. I only hoped that Brooke wasn't about to tell me that she and Isaac were now new best friends. I mean, it wasn't like you could claim custody over your friends or anything, but I'd like to think that she was gonna stay my best friend and not leave me for a boy. A girl never likes to see the day when she becomes second to her best friend's new boyfriend. You would think that was the problem I had with the Untouchables. If only. With them, it was a lot more than that. I wish it were that simple— fighting over who got to spend more time with them, me or their boyfriends. That kind of problem was easy to resolve. But what they did? That was something so hard to fix I didn't know if even Einstein would know what to do. But I had to stop thinking about that. I had the rest of health class and the rest of the day to get through. The fact of the matter was, Brooke and Isaac were both not in school. And I just had to deal with it whether I liked it or not. It could have been just a coincidence.

I had never been this excited for the bell to ring, signaling the end of the day before. Maybe on the last day of school? The anticipation of what I was about to find out kept me on edge. Part of me, throughout the day, kept thinking that she'd show up eventually; she was just gonna show up late. But when Brooke didn't show up and neither did Isaac, I was left waiting for the bell to ring.

When the bell finally rang I dashed out the door like one of those cottontail rabbits from my childhood. I sped the whole way home, and when I finally pulled into the driveway, I saw it. There was Brooke's car! Yes! She was home! Then I figured that Mom and Dad weren't home, but that Lina

215

was. Luckily, Brooke and I didn't have a shift at Co~Z Monster either. I didn't even have to unlock the door; it practically burst open of its own volition. Brooke threw her arms around me and gave me a great big hug. I was blown away, but I was also confused. She had only been gone for one night and one day. It wasn't like she had been gone for ten years and she was my long lost sister or anything. I was an only child after all. I didn't have sibling feelings.

Oh she was good. She knew it was hard to be angry with someone who gives you a great big hug. Because it was hard. It's like they say, "kill them with kindness." I had no idea who said that, but it made sense. Sometimes it was hard to fight back when someone was so nice to you. You couldn't help it. You really didn't have a choice. It was like when you were watching someone break down and cry right in front of you, you couldn't just stand there and ignore them like it wasn't happening. Even the most cold-hearted woman couldn't stand by and watch someone cry on the floor and not want to reach out or do anything about it. It was not possible. You really didn't have a choice in this situation either.

I wasn't, however, about to let her do that. I needed answers. I was sure Lina had already attacked her with a million questions, but I couldn't help it! People couldn't just go missing on me and not tell me why or what happened. Maybe it was okay in her world, but it wasn't okay in mine and I was starting to feel like Revelation was about to repeat itself. Inside my twisted stomach, I wasn't feeling well. A girl can only lose so many friends at once. Losing more right away would just not be safe for her health, both physically and mentally. While I was no doctor, nor did I have the brain capacity to hold the information it would take to get into medical school, I did know what would happen if Brooke kept hiding information from me and cutting me off. She hadn't gone to extremes yet, but my brain was telling me that she might. I knew there was a lot for her to handle, but at the same time, there was an equal amount for me to handle, too. Weren't we all going through a lot? Like always? Wasn't that just life?

"I'm so glad you're back, but what happened? Why'd you take off like that? Where did you go? Everyone was so worried, I can't believe it!" Now it was my turn to be out of breath. I had a myriad of questions for her and I was sure if I kept going at it, I would never finish and I'd be asking her these questions for the rest of our lives.

Brooke pulled me inside quickly and shut the door before our conversation escalated and we started attracting the attention of the neighbors. It wasn't like I cared what they thought, but you know, it was just not exactly a good thing to broadcast your problems to the world while knowing that Brooke wasn't just any other girl. I knew this, yet I still started yelling at her out in the open. You lose your head sometimes when you've been worried sick and who's who just doesn't matter anymore. Only in my case, it did. Aarrgggh! To be stuck in such a quandary!

"Amber, you're home!" Lina cried out loud. "Don't mind me, I'll leave you two girls to talk!"

Something was really strange. Either Mrs. Fulton was simply too happy to see her daughter home to be mad or she was out of her mind. Her voice was different...she was acting all sweet...not her usual self.

I tried to brush it off as her just being happy to see her daughter. That was the only explanation I could come up with. As far as I knew, nothing else had changed about Lina. She was acting so girlish, though. It was kind of pathetic. I hated mothers who

219

automatically assumed that all girls liked girl talk and doing their hair and makeup and all that jazz. I wasn't one of those girls. Those girlish things seemed so, so trivial and pointless. I just never got involved in them. I wasn't a tomboy and I wasn't a feminist or anything, but I found girly girls and anything to do with being a girly girl kind of annoying. I mean, in a way I could see why Brooke hated chick flicks. They weren't real. They always featured some girl who couldn't get her crush to notice her because her hair was too curly or she wore glasses and then one day she straightens her hair and gets contacts and bam! her crush is into her. They were suggesting that the only way you can get your crush to notice you is if you change everything about the way you look. Some of the "better" ones inserted some random best guy friend who has been noticing the main girl character all along, but has to keep quiet about his feelings because she lusts after some other guy who happens to be a lot cooler than he is. She learns a lesson, realizes that her best guy friend is really the guy for her, and then ends up with him instead of her original crush. I mean, seriously, come on now. Just thinking about some of those movies was enough to make me a bit sick to my stomach (not literally!).

I didn't hate girly girls, I just got turned off sometimes when people assumed all girls cared about were looks and nothing else.

For now, though, I had to get my head back into what was important: what did Brooke do and with whom? Where was she yesterday and why wasn't she in school? As usual, we went into our room and this time I watched Brooke sit down on the floor as she talked all about yesterday.

What I suspected was half-true. She and Isaac were friends now, but she hadn't told me. She said that she was really upset the day before and by the time I had started

221

asking her questions at work, she was ready to fly off. She didn't want to be in the same room, under the same roof, as Lina, for one more second. So when Lina entered the house, she had to drive off. That was all she had. And really, since becoming friends with Isaac, he was the only person she could go to. They hung out during breaks and even a little bit after work when I wasn't there. Of course, he always knew her as Sally Hunter, not anyone else—she hadn't revealed her identity. That was one good thing. But she and Isaac were now all buddy-buddy and all? That was weird! She had been sneaking around behind my back getting to know him, huh? And I couldn't believe she thought I'd have a problem with it! It made me think she had her own secret motive because it seemed to me anyone who couldn't tell me to my face what was going on secretly wanted to change something about me or themselves without including me in on it. Was she up to something or just trying to meet a new face here besides the Untouchables? For one thing, I admired that she didn't take everything at face value. She wasn't gullible. She liked to meet people herself and make her own judgments about them, without taking other people's word for it. For another thing, she really had guts to hide a relationship with someone from her family and friends. Maybe he was more than what he seemed.

We all have our initial judgments of people when we first meet them, but oftentimes we don't take the time to look past what is on the cover and dig beneath the surface. How typical. I wondered how long their friendship had been going on and how much hanging out they had done without me. It must have been a lot if they felt comfortable enough with each other to have sleepovers. What exactly had they been talking about anyway, since she couldn't reveal too much? And the all-important question of all: did they like each other now?

I had heard that some of the best romantic relationships started from great friendships. I was wondering, as Brooke went on about her night, if that was what was happening between her and Isaac. And no, I didn't have other complicated feelings. That was the only thought I had in mind. If she really wanted things to work out as more than just friends with him, it was fine by me, no questions asked. That was how I really felt. In some ways, Brooke was gushing about her time spent with Isaac in a schoolgirl crush kind of way. She still wouldn't admit that she liked hanging out with him, let alone that she liked him. Aii-ya! Such is the tragedy of teen love.

Now that my attention was diverted, I was less upset with Brooke and more interested in her love life. Oddly.

"Brooke, are you sure you don't just...

you know...*like* Isaac?"

Brooke looked appalled. "No, of course not! Why would you suspect such a thing?"

That was weird. For someone who enjoyed being friends with him, Brooke was acting like being with Isaac was the last thing on her mind. This new development was getting way out of hand. I couldn't help but think that perhaps Brooke was masking her feelings for Isaac because she still thought I liked Isaac. She said she had hidden the fact she'd been hanging out with him because she was afraid I'd get upset. Maybe it was that transference thing people talked about. She secretly liked him and she was trying to push it off on me so I wouldn't notice how much she liked him.

Why would I get upset?! For some reason, I was a bit unsettled at the thought that Brooke kept thinking I had a thing for Isaac. It seemed so silly to imagine actually liking someone that it seemed even more ridiculous that Brooke couldn't leave the subject alone, taunting me at every chance she got. What was her problem anyway? She could be so nice and generous with her talent for one second and then the next second she could be so…so….oooh….evil! She could let every other thing go, but not this obsession over whether Isaac and I had chemistry or not. Please don't tell me that she decided to become best friends with him just to set us up or something. How humiliating that would be. I didn't know why girls tortured each other like this. We could be so silly sometimes. And absolutely ruthless.

Frustrated, I responded, "Because you're so excited every time you talk about him and he was the first person you thought of when you needed a place to crash even though you aren't dating. I mean, come on, hell-llloooo! You could have asked any of your new girl friends, but you asked *him*."

"Is there a problem asking him or something? Are you *sure* you're not the one with a crush on Isaac?" Brooke retorted.

"So you're saying that this whole emergency getaway thing wasn't just an excuse to spend a night at your new so-called boy 'just friends' house? You're saying that—" I didn't get to finish.

"Seriously, Amber? Seriously? I'm having a quarter-life crisis and all you can think about is if Sally Hunter is secretly hooking up with 'hot senior guy' from Mr. Kurt's health class? Seriously?" Brooke interrupted, a flat expression on her face.

"You said that three times already," I said.

"No, I haven't! What have I said three times?"

"Seriously," I answered, trying not to laugh. Glad to know that Brooke Fulton was back in the building.

Brooke started cracking up.

We decided then and there that whoever liked Isaac or didn't like Isaac wouldn't matter. What did matter was getting back on track. Getting this demo out and getting life straightened out the best way that two teenage girls knew how—have a pajama-movie-marathon party, just us girls. Well, we were going to do that as soon as midterms were over and it was time for Christmas break. Wasn't it crazy how Christmas break was so soon after Thanksgiving break? It was so nice…and a bit scary at the same time. Gosh, and this was gonna sound terrible, but just like kids everywhere, we basically only cared about Christmas because of the break we got from school. Just like when it snows: it's great for us, but bad for everyone else. Snow days!

Before we let the topic drop, though, Brooke explained to me how she really felt about Isaac so that, whatever the case may be, we were at least honest with each other about that. She insisted that she wasn't into him as more than a friend. The way she liked to do things was simple: get to be friends with guys first, then assess their romantic potential. If they have no romantic potential, then at least she'd gained another friend who could share her secrets from the male point of view, which upped her game and gave her a better shot at her real crush.

Wow. For a girl who was going through a quarter-life crisis, I'd say she was really prepared in the dating department. I wasn't even sure how my parents felt about it, considering that they were constantly fighting and all, but if I had to guess I'd say that they'd rather I didn't date, but if I did, they wouldn't kill him or anything. I supposed it wasn't all that great of a positive response, but it was the best I could expect from two people who were having marital issues and were both related to me.

I wasn't gonna ask anymore. I was just going to trust her. It seemed like she had a good point. I was going to keep that little tidbit in mind as a piece of good advice, even though my experience with guys was limited: slim to none. Not that I cared. I had plenty of other things on my mind to keep myself occupied. There were many other much more important things to worry about in the world than what some stupid boy thought of me and how I looked.

It seemed that the I'm-not-sure-I-like-Isaac saga would continue for at least a little while longer. It was funny. At work, he was nice and talked to us, but during class, he acted like he didn't really know us at all. To me that was kind of strange, considering that Brooke insisted that they were good friends, after all. Shouldn't good friends at least acknowledge each other's existence in class? Or had I missed something? It seemed that it hadn't bothered Brooke because he had been that way from the very beginning and he was still that way now, so nothing had changed. When we all worked together, it was awesome. I had heard somewhere that guys could never be "just friends" with a girl, but Isaac seemed to be the exception to this rule. He was, amazingly, holding up his end of the deal and almost never crossed the line. Knowing that he and Brooke were pretty close friends now, for some reason, made me more comfortable around him and more free to be myself around him, whatever that was. I was starting to get the hang of things, almost believing that I was building a three-way friendship with them, a la Lizzie McGuire. Hm-hmmm. Wasn't that going to be just dandy? Was this really happening? Or was I just making things up as I went along?

I always had a fear that my brain was spontaneously making things up in whatever I was doing. I would be pulled into some sort of fantasy and when I snapped out of it, everything would look so sad and disappointing. I guess Dickens was right: it was better not to have such high expectations. Or maybe fantasy was just better than reality and I simply preferred to live in it. Living in what you thought the world was like was so much more inviting than what the world was actually like. Less scary that way too.

For a long time the manager at Co~Z Monster had us working different shifts, which meant that even though we were all working, we almost never had our breaks at the exact same time, all three together. It was usually two at a time, sometimes one at a time, which was a little less fun. But I was really adjusting to working alongside Isaac. It wasn't as difficult to get used to as I had imagined. Even with my little experience talking to guys, I found that as long as we were always around each other, I could become comfortable talking to him. He may have been a senior, but he was still human. Once I got that thought into my head, it was a whole lot easier to be myself around him.

It wasn't that I had been nervous around him because I liked him or something like that. It was just that I wasn't the most comfortable, well-articulated person around people I didn't know very well, especially people of the opposite sex. And it wasn't just my lack of experience interacting with boys; it was the thought that interacting with boys could lead to relationships and that was something I wasn't sure I was ready for.

Getting into relationships seemed to be so easy for my peers, but it never seemed possible for me. Did they just not take it as seriously as I did? Did they only care about the physical parts about being in a relationship and not the rest, the important parts that made a relationship a relationship? Did they not care who they were, who they were striving to become? I wondered how some kids my age could not know what they wanted out of life and who they were as people, yet they knew who they wanted to be with. In addition, that person was okay with the fact that this new boyfriend/girlfriend didn't know much about life. That was what puzzled me the most about relationships and interactions with the opposite sex. How was dealing with uncertainty okay? Or did all those things that I constantly worried about just not matter to those people? It was no secret that I had a lot of questions on my mind, but try as I might, I couldn't make them go away. They hung in the air, like a hot-air balloon, and wouldn't float down until I either didn't worry about them anymore or, lo and behold, I found an answer for them. Then I had one last moment with them, and they were out of the hot-air balloon and floating up, up, into the clouds like helium balloons. Some day some astronaut is going to find a whole bunch of helium balloons full of my worries and wonder where they came from.

Co~Z Monster had a special break room where employees could go when on break from a shift. It was at the back of the shop, behind the tables where people sat when they wanted to be secluded from everyone else for a change.

Right next door to the break room were our lockers. Yes, it was so silly. We had yet another set of lockers for work as well. Including school, I now had three locker combinations to remember: my homeroom locker, my gym locker, and now my Co~Z Monster locker. These were our employee lockers where we could store our personal belongings before getting started on our shift. I usually tried not to bring anything too personal. Just the essentials. Though I hadn't been here for long, I suspected that a lot of drama went down in the employee locker room. It made me feel like I was a part of something. And that made me feel good.

After a while of us being on different shifts, our manager started putting Isaac and me on the same breaks, so I found myself alone with him in the break room a lot. Well, if you didn't count the other employees that on occasion got grouped in with us as well. It was nice this way because whenever Dad was there, it felt awkward. He usually worked the morning shifts and we worked the afternoon shifts, so working the same shifts as Dad didn't come up often. During those breaks with Isaac, I liked to think of them as our time. We weren't a couple or anything, but it was nice to get to know Isaac without Sally there. It killed me that he didn't know who Sally really was and would most likely never get to. It was getting harder and harder to hold that information back. But I promised myself that I wouldn't tell him, even as tempting as it was to do so.

One day Isaac was a few minutes late getting to the break room, so I had those blessed few minutes to myself. I pulled out the draft of the lyrics to my demo that I had been working so hard on the last few weeks. I took out a pencil from my green Co~Z Monster apron and started crossing out some of the words, scratching at the parchment, trying to come up with the words that would represent Amber Yang, me. Then Isaac walked in to the break room, carrying a coffee cup. I wasn't surprised. It was not news that as valued employees of Co~Z Monster we were allowed free coffees when someone messed up an order, so for him to walk in with an extra cup wasn't so big a deal. But then he stopped by where I was sitting and placed the cup in front of me.

"Amber, it's a tall vanilla latte," he said.

My mouth dropped open. Wha-aaa— aaa—? That's what I wanted to say. What I said was, "How did you—???" I know, it wasn't much better, but I wasn't used to people doing me any favors, especially not boys. This was a first.

"Don't worry about it," Isaac said. How

could he be so nonchalant? This clearly wasn't some mistake drink. Vanilla lattes were my favorite. Did he sneak it past the manager? What would happen if the manager found out—would he get fired? How could he tell me not to worry?

Maybe I was overreacting again. It's just that I had so much I wanted to ask and so much I wanted to say to him. Instead, I said nothing and took a sip. The latte was *good*. It tasted especially warm and fuzzy. "Thank you," I said.

"You're welcome," he replied. Then he glanced over at what was in front of me. "What's that you're working on?" he asked.

I looked back down at my lyrics. There was still no title as of yet. I covered the paper with my hand. "Nothing," I said quickly. I was getting comfortable with hanging around Isaac, but not *that* comfortable. Just like Sally wasn't about to call herself Brooke, artist Amber wasn't about to call herself singer Amber. Not yet.

"That's not nothing," he countered. "When people say that, it's just code for 'I'm working on something that could possibly change my life, but I'm afraid it's not going to work out so I don't want to show it to you.'" He paused, then added, "Am I right?"

Wow. Nailed it. But I wasn't about to let him off the hook so easily. I started to put two and two together about those Wednesday and Saturday shifts he kept missing. "Well, that depends. Are you secretly on the basketball team?"

He gave a weird look that said, what are you talking about? "Where'd you get that idea?"

Did he really not remember that time at the Hope Court? Maybe he really was oblivious. "Ha, never mind." I didn't know if basketball was an appropriate subject to broach with Isaac. After all, he might have shown his soft side when he made me my favorite drink, but he was still Mr.

Opinionated. That was not about to change any time soon.

His face changed. "No, really. You can tell me, you know," he said. I don't know what prompted this sudden change, but I decided that if he was willing to open up, then I had to be willing to do the same.

"I've seen you at the Hoop," I said.

His eyebrows lifted. I wondered what that meant for him. Then he responded, "Oh, that's nothing. I just like a pickup every now and then with my friends, you know?"

I smiled. "You said 'nothing'!" Checkmate.

Isaac hit his fist on the table lightly and laughed. "Darn!"

I took another sip of my drink. "So you gonna tell me what this basketball thing is all about or what?"

He didn't say anything at first. I could tell he was seriously debating how much information he wanted to disclose to me in the break room. It reminded me of the night of Revelation. The look on his face was a lot like the one Karen was wearing that night. Karen looked so confused and unsure of what she had to tell me, like she was torn between doing the right thing and doing the thing that she knew would hurt me, would expose herself as a traitor, but she had to do anyway. She proceeded to do the latter. She told me all about the rumors that she and Serena had been spreading about me as well as what she said about my dad. Yes, that he was cheating on my mom with some younger woman and that I had "been with" some guy on the basketball team. I had no idea which one, J.V. or V. or even which guy, and I had no idea about the cheating part with my dad nor the name of the woman if it was true. It was true, however, that Mom wanted a permanent separation from Dad, and while I'd always suspected there was another reason besides the fact they argued all the time, I'd never believe that he'd do something like that to her. In that moment, when my so-called best friends revealed their true colors, I couldn't help but be selfish. How could they give me a bad rep for something I didn't do, when everyone knows for a fact that I could have never been that girl who just gives it up to some jock at school? They knew that I had never so much as held hands with a boy, let alone spent the night with one. How could they? What could possibly make them say such horrible things? Oh man, sitting across from Isaac I may have been finally acting rationally again, but that night, which became Revelation, was not a night for acting rationally for sure. It was an end to two best friendships that had started years before Revelation.

Secrets could bring girls together, it was true. Well, obviously it was or Karen and Serena wouldn't have found a new crew to roll with after spreading all that dirt around.

Later I found out they had been put up to it to get in with this new group of friends. Whatever made them decide to stoop that low was beyond my comprehension; I knew deep down in the bottom of my heart that they were better than that. Life is a lot like wedding vows: we have to live through it whether it's for better or for worse. Some people choose to change for the better and others choose to change for the worse, but I'd like to believe that even those who change for the worse will eventually realize their mistakes and change for the better.

I had never been to a wedding before, but that's what I thought a typical American wedding was supposed to be like. When Mom and Dad got married, they didn't have one of those weddings with vows and such. They did, however, have a party at a friend's house, one where Lina was invited—back when they were still in touch, before Lina was married. Life seemed like it should be lived out like a wedding ceremony. You are supposed to be happy with the relationships you are a part of and you are not supposed to betray those relationships because that is just simply, quite frankly, wrong. To say that after Karen revealed the truth to my face I felt like my heart had just been ripped out of my chest and put into a blender before the shredded remains were poured into a glass, would have been an understatement. I lost that safety, that trust that night. They say to forgive and forget, but unfortunately, while I'll probably be able to do the first eventually, I know that I won't ever be able to do the second, no matter how hard I try.

Secrets could also tear girls apart. I just never thought that the same secrets that would bring one set of girls together could tear another set of girls apart. The people at school were afraid of more than just my new rep, though. Besides the fact that it was so unlike me, no one wanted to be associated with an easy girl. Of that I was sure. I just didn't think Karen and Serena had predicted what the ramifications of their rumors would be. I bet they didn't think it through, didn't think they would end up isolating me. Was I hurt? Of course. But I wasn't going to let this get the best of me, even if at first it seemed I had.

Back in the break room, Isaac started to talk about his hidden basketball talent and how he was hoping he could be a walk-on in college, then he stopped himself. Whether he could tell that I wasn't giving him my full attention or not I would never have a clue, but I could tell it was not information he really wanted to divulge to me right that second. I mean, I had caught the poor boy off guard. It was amazing that he was not affected by all the gossip and rumors about me. I never gave him proper credit. There was nothing I could give him, except maybe the truth.

"So what are you working on? What is

that?" Isaac asked, trying to change the subject.

I decided to be honest and direct. "A song. I'm writing a song," I said.

"Oh, that's awesome. I didn't know you were into music," he remarked, surprised.

"Yeah, me too," I said.

Now he gave me a questioning glance. "You too? You didn't know you were into music?"

I have to admit, I was surprised at my own choice of words. What made me think for a second that I wasn't sure about being into music? Well, that was obvious, considering my mixed feelings about this upcoming demo, but even from the time I was very little I loved to sing. I mean, let's face it, I had started and quit many things in the past, but the one thing I couldn't stop myself from doing no matter what was happening was singing. That was the reason I wanted to make it my career. So if I was so sure about my passion for music, why couldn't I say so in front of other people? I had no qualms about voicing my opinions with Brooke, but I couldn't even tell my parents yet. Did I somehow have to pretend that I didn't know this about myself?

"Well, no. Let's just say I didn't think I'd ever find myself scribbling away on a piece of paper trying to write the lyrics to a brand-new hit song," I said.

"A brand-new hit song? Is that right?" Isaac said.

"Well, I don't know about that, but I hope so." I looked down. Suddenly I wasn't feeling so hot. I didn't know what it was, almost embarrassed, I guess. I didn't even know why.

"Amber," Isaac said, firmly. "Do you want to be a singer?" He asked me softly, but not in any judgmental sort of way, like he just wanted to know the truth, to know what I was hiding.

I bit my lip, still not looking at him, though I could feel his eyes on me. I nodded my head, or at least, I tried to nod.

Then I felt Isaac touch my arm as he said, a little more audibly this time, "That's great, Amber."

I chose that moment to look up at him. It felt weird to have his hand there. No boy had ever touched me before, not even playfully as a joke. I wasn't a prude or anything, I just didn't really have many chances with the opposite sex, especially after the rumors were spread. I thought this whole situation was kind of funny, though. I mean, the whole school was operating under the idea that promiscuity was okay for girls who gave it up already and continued to give it up, but when one goody-goody girl was rumored to have given it up all of a sudden it was OMG! let's halt the presses and put in that extra snippet. You know, I had a right to be angry at this. At the fact that it was not okay for a little miss goody-two-shoes to do anything wrong, but it was perfectly fine for the rest of the student population. I mean, granted all that stuff about me wasn't true, but just the fact that schools operated under this notion spoke volumes about what everyone thought of you if you gave it up. Seriously. This was getting ridiculous. Maybe I should have just not cared. But how easy was that going to be?

And now I had to deal with a boy touching my arm for the first time. It wasn't scary, I just wasn't expecting it. "Really? Is it? You really think singing is a good step for me?" I asked him tentatively.

Then he let go. "Yeah, it's great to finally see you want something for a change," he said, sounding so sure of himself.

"Hey, what's that supposed to mean?"

"It means that all year long I've seen you take second seat behind Sally, letting her speak up for the both of you, never going for what you want."

"That's not fair. She sits next to me," I protested.

"Ha," Isaac let out, like he'd been suppressing a laugh this whole conversation. "Okay, maybe I haven't been fair. I'm glad you can take this lightly, though." He smiled.

Then I couldn't help but laugh too.

Before we knew it, break was over and I found myself chattering with him about how he had an opinion about everything, and that I had noticed that about him the first time we had to work together on a group assignment. I found that to be a pretty bold move, telling a boy what I had noticed the first time we met, but with Isaac, it was really easy to talk. That was strange, considering my history with boys. We were walking out of the break room together, and I found myself laughing at Isaac's jokes and lightly tapping him on the arm when I thought he was making fun of something I said. I didn't realize what it must have looked like to Brooke until I saw her eyes boring into mine as we walked by her on the way back to the counter. She was just getting off for her break and though she gave me a smile, I noticed that it was a crooked one, not warm and inviting like her usual cheery self.

When work was over and we were in my car, we drove home in silence. Brooke wasn't interested in talking. This time, instead of asking, I knew better and remained silent.

We walked into the living room. There was a huge, puffy yellow envelope on the wooden cocktail table in the center of the room. Uh-oh. This couldn't be good. Mom had been waiting for weeks for those divorce papers to finally come in the mail. I didn't know what they would look like when they came, but I had a strange feeling that that yellow envelope in the center of the room probably held them hostage inside. I also had a feeling that Mom had been having trouble with this whole divorce thing from the very beginning. I mean, why had she waited for almost a year before requesting the papers in the mail? If she hadn't waited, what had taken them so long to arrive? I knew from overhearing their arguments that she had been questioning her decision all along. But now that the papers were finally here, what did that mean? Was that her final answer? Suddenly I felt like I was watching my mom on *Who Wants to Be a Millionaire?* and she was down to her final lifeline or something. She'd already phoned a friend, polled the audience, and narrowed the answers down to 50/50. Regis Philbin was asking her, while she was sitting in the hot seat, if a permanent separation from her husband was her final answer and the nerve-wracking beating was booming over the intercom, making my heart race along with it, as I waited for her to give him a final yes or no. This was it. Inside that envelope lay the answer to our future as a family. It was too much to process at once, but eventually I would have to come to terms with it. For the moment, standing there looking at it was too much to bear.

I felt like crying, but I didn't. I knew that this wasn't the time or place. That envelope meant that Mom was home already, as she was the one who picked up the mail every day and I wasn't ready for her to see me break down over a stupid envelope. I refused to believe it was over. It couldn't be over! This was our life and I was gonna take a stand!

Brooke had already left for our room and closed the door. She still hadn't said anything and I was fine with that. I think we both needed some alone time anyway.

"Hey, Isaac," Sally said.

It was all weird. She wasn't acting herself again and I couldn't help but wonder if she was always so dramatic. This couldn't be the real Brooke Fulton. The real Brooke Fulton had changed since she had moved to our house. That much was certain.

Sally punched me in the arm. "Ow!" I yelled out, trying not to be too loud. "What was that for?"

"Say hi to him," she whispered through clenched teeth.

I really marveled at this new behavior. Was

she bipolar or something? Was this her being melancholy time? Isaac walked by and did his usual "Hello, ladies" bit before flashing us his smile. I noticed Sally smiling back and all I could say was, "Hi." Then Isaac walked to the back of the shop, into the employee locker room. Sally punched me in the arm again, this time a bit harder.

"What is wrong with you?" I asked, a bit aggravated.

"What's wrong with me? What's wrong with me? That boy totally digs you and you can barely say more than one word to him when he walks by!" She paused, waiting for me to say something, anything in return. But I said nothing. So she continued. "I have been holding back my feelings for him this whole time, listening to him talk about you, say how much he likes to come to work so he can get close to you and have the chance to get to know you better…"

So she finally admitted her feelings. Why

she was so mad at me about it I really didn't understand. I tuned her out. The rest of the shift was awkward.

By the time we were ready to go, I couldn't wait. Considering how well I had been settling in at Co~Z Monster, that was unusual, though I suppose not entirely unexpected. In one work shift Sally had managed to blow me right out of my comfort zone. Single-handedly, I might add, not that it matters. Not only was I freaked out about Isaac possibly, maybe liking me, but I also didn't know what to make of Sally. When was Brooke going to re-inhabit her body? I was waiting for just Brooke to come back.

I waited until we were out of earshot of Isaac before starting. "What was that? What was that all about? How could you force me to bump into him so many times?!"

"I said I was sorry," Brooke said indignantly.

"What's gotten into you? One minute you're all happy and ready to go, figured

255

out what you want to do with your life, and the next minute you're back to not knowing anything about anything and acting like the only thing that matters is what boy you date!" Ugh. I hated confrontations. I hated being the one confronting even more.

I doubted anyone really secretly loved confrontations. Unless they were one of those people who always found themselves in an altercation of some kind and loved to get all up in each other's faces, shouting until someone won and someone got hurt. Yeah, unless they were that kind of person, I highly doubted that anyone loved confrontations.

But here I was, in a confrontation.

"Oh, at least I'm not afraid to make a move!"

"What's that supposed to mean?" I wondered if we were finally going to make our true confessions or some derivative of that.

"What that means is how come there's a cute senior guy available and totally, completely interested in you and you don't even budge?"

"Maybe I'm not interested in getting into a relationship right now. Plus, I thought you said that being friends with someone first is better than jumping into a relationship whenever the chance arrives."

I guess Brooke didn't want the argument to escalate into a full-fledged fight because she didn't respond at first. We were still in the parking lot. She held onto my arms and looked me dead in the eye. "Amber, there is so much more to life than just what you want to be."

Was she being serious? That seemed to be the only thing on her mind these last few weeks and now all of a sudden, she's changing her mind?

"You're only young once. Take some time to fall in love," she continued. Why did she sound like a mother? Yes, I say a mother because mine would have never given me advice like that. Mine would have told me to find myself first, figure out what I wanted to do with the rest of my life, and then, then fall in love.

"All right, this is enough philosophizing

for one day. Let's go home," I said, trying to put my foot down and an end to her crazy notions, as sound as they may have seemed. When is falling in love ever planned? Of course, I could avoid it altogether by not obsessing with girls and not talking to any guys who could be potential boyfriends. So I could put it off, but didn't the heart want what the heart wanted? Wasn't that how it worked every single time?

"Whatever," Brooke said, rolling her eyes.

Where was this attitude coming from? It felt like I was dealing with a petulant child all of a sudden when before I admired Brooke for being one of the most mature girls I knew. She had only been here a few months. We were coming up on Christmas and she had changed so much. Was that what happened when someone got a wee taste of fame? For Brooke, it was so much more than a wee bit. Maybe that was the problem.

OIL IN THE WOK

Maybe it was because it was the holiday season or maybe it was because people usually cooled off after a few days, but after a week or so Brooke had completely dropped the subject of Isaac and had gone back to her normal self again, for which I was very grateful. We were now officially done with writing the song; it was time to record it. Yay! Things were also back to normal at Co~Z Monster. We were now serving our special holiday coffee, complete with green whipped cream and a sprinkling of cinnamon on top. Isaac and I had been talking as good old buddies, not too many heart-to-hearts like we used to in the break room. I thought he was sensing that I didn't want to get too close to him or start anything because he had completely stopped touching my arm or joking around too much.

That didn't bother me, though. It was really okay. After thinking about it some more, without Brooke pestering me all the time, I decided I didn't have feelings for him. Was it normal to be like this? I had no idea, but we always had to keep going because that was all we could do.

Luckily for me, ever since I started working at Co~Z Monster, Karen and Serena had reduced the number of their visits. So far they hadn't even noticed my new position behind the counter. If they came in, I was either on my break or in the bathroom or suddenly felt the need to stop by the back of the shop for something. They always missed me. Yes, I was pitifully avoiding them, but it would have been so awkward to have them run into me here. I was sure of that.

And then it happened. I was working the register one day, not expecting much, and Isaac was working the orders. Then the door opened and in walked Karen, with Serena trailing a few feet behind her. Oh, boy. I didn't know what to do. Not for the first time, I really didn't know how I was going to get myself out of this one. So I did what every mature girl would have done in this situation to patch up a beautiful friendship from the past: I ducked.

And then I dropped to the floor, hiding behind the counter. For added drama, I covered my face with my hands. I hoped beyond hope that neither Karen nor Serena had seen me. There was no way I was going to be having any contact with the Untouchables. Not today. Not ever!

Anger is like a fire-breathing dragon that lives inside your stomach. It gets warmer and warmer, ready to spew forth a full blast of fire from the belly once its wrath is unleashed. Yes, I knew that holding grudges was unhealthy and it may be only a girl thing, but I couldn't help myself. Once that dragon was in, I couldn't stop it from getting released.

Everyone knows that an unreleased dragon will just get a bigger belly.

That was how I felt about the Untouchables every time I thought of them. My dragon's belly was always armed and ready. Like that evil black dragon from *Sleeping Beauty* that the evil witch sets on Aurora, my fire was ready to destroy everything in its path, given the chance. The sound of their names made me cringe. I didn't want to cause a scene in the middle of the shop, but it looked like it was too late for that.

"Amber! Amber! What's wrong?" I felt Isaac shaking me. I wondered if he recognized the Untouchables. "We have customers." Apparently not. "What are you doing?" Now he was prying my hands open. I could see him out of the corner of my right eye. Above me I heard, "We'll be with you in just a moment." Then I heard, "Is that Amber?" I knew the voice belonged to Serena. Serena. How dare she?! She had spoken my name as if we were still buddy-buddy, but at the same time, with a questioning tone, as if she wasn't sure if she should be saying my name at all. I knew I should maybe be more merciful or more forgiving or something, but even with the time that had passed, I couldn't find it in my heart to just let Revelation drop.

Time was up. That was how it seemed. I could avoid her at school and I could avoid her at home, but it seemed that I could not, no matter how I tried, avoid her at Co~Z Monster.

"Okay, do you want to tell me what's up?" Isaac asked. He was stooping down, speaking quietly. When I didn't answer, he said, "You know what, we don't have time for this. I don't know what's going on, but I can only assume it's got something to do with your past, something you've never told me before. Obviously you know these girls and obviously you don't want to face them. I'm guessing you've been hiding from them for a while. Whatever it is, for the sake of work and for this coffee shop, could you please get your act together and serve these next few girls? If you do, I promise I will do whatever you want after this shift is over to make it up to you." Isaac paused for breath, expecting me to say something in return. When I didn't, he added, "Please? Co~Z Monster is counting on you!"

Somehow I managed to slowly uncover my eyes with both my hands. Isaac smiled. He smiled like that time when he brought me a tall vanilla latte. It was a magical smile. I know it's silly, but sometimes a girl who has been relationship-deprived misses a nice smile. He gave me his hand. I gave him mine. He helped me up to a standing position. Well, at least something that resembled a standing position. So far, my green-aproned back was facing the Untouchables, assuming they were still waiting there.

An idea popped into my head as I was standing there, looking at the wall.

I turned around and faced Karen and

Serena. I didn't say anything. I let them say, "Amber!" I didn't respond. I didn't even pay attention to the tones of their voices.

I had learned a long time ago that people's tone of voice could tell you a lot about their mood. Like, if they were fading out and sounding weak, they were probably sleepy and really tired. Okay, maybe that didn't count as a tone. But say their voice was firm and strong. That might mean they were angry or ready to talk about something serious. If they were speaking in loud, excited tones, they were probably either frustrated or bursting with news about something really good that had just happened to them. If they were speaking in low, mumbling tones, then I could guess that they were sad or disappointed about something that they had been really looking forward to. These were basic things that probably anyone could have picked up on, but they really clued me in on stuff that was important.

I usually paid close attention to details like this, so it was definitely a first that when the Untouchables were addressing me, I didn't try to read them. I didn't even look up from the counter. I pulled out a pen from my apron pocket, grabbed the closest Co~Z Monster brown napkin, and put both on the counter in front of the girls. Then, I finally spoke.

"Put your order on this napkin," I said, in as steady a voice I could muster. I didn't look up at them.

"Amber, we're sorry," I heard Karen's voice say, firmly but with a bit of a shake in there.

I stopped what I was doing for a minute. I decided I wasn't going to be fooled. I stared at the register screen, racking my brain for any memories of the days when me and the Untouchables would come into this exact coffee shop and we each ordered our favorite drink. When I got the napkin back, I wanted to know that I could accurately predict which drinks I'd have to punch in. But try as I might,

I found that part of my memory weak. It was amazing how much I remembered from the night of Revelation, yet I couldn't remember the most basic, simple specifics of my old friends. Man, Isaac was right *again*. I had been spending too much time on this. You couldn't change the past, but you could make some changes in the present to hope for a different future. Hopefully a better one. Either way, if you put some effort in the present, you can make a change for your future.

When Karen passed me the napkin, I punched in one tall black Americano and one tall Death by Chocolate. Wow. That wasn't what I had guessed. They didn't look familiar at all. Did I know these girls anymore?

Apparently not. They seemed to have changed their favorite drinks, probably to fit in with their new crowd. What was that popular girl's name? Sherry? Janine? It didn't matter. They were now a part of Mariella's group or whatever her name was. I supposed

Mariella liked to drink Americanos.

Karen remained quiet. Serena, however, decided that now would be a good time for an apology. Great. There were some good points about that girl, if I dug deep enough into my brain, but perfect timing was not one of them.

"Amber, we're really sorry. We were stupid. We really shouldn't have told anyone anything…" As Serena went on and on about how sorry she was, I continued to stare at anything except her face. I had been stewing for months and months about what she had done, trying to figure out what I wanted from them. Never in a thousand years did I want to hear an apology from the queen of bad news herself. What I wanted was for her to take everything back. What I wanted was for her never to have said anything in the first place. I didn't want her apology. I didn't want her to come here, feeling sorry for me. I wanted her to turn out to be a genuinely good faithful loyal friend instead of what she really was: a betraying backstabbing manipulative disrespectful…

We both knew it was too late to go back. There was no use pining for something that couldn't be. Sometimes, no matter how embarrassing the situation, we must carry on with as much strength as we can muster. It isn't always easy and often we need some time to heal so that the past can finally be put in the past, but when we do, we can be sure to lift our heads up again.

Though the shop was very nearly empty at the moment, whatever I wanted would have to wait because I didn't want to cause a scene. That, my friends, would have been very unbecoming. It was funny that no matter what was going on, I was still watching out for decorum. For that reason, I kept quiet. I didn't want them to think I was going to accept an apology that easily. It took them this long and only when they suddenly had the urge to stop by Co~Z Monster and found me working there? Did they really think a few sorry words would erase the pain? Would make everything okay? Was that it? Was this supposed to make them feel less guilty for what they had done?

I know, I was having a moment. A moment where it seemed that bad things were happening to me and no one else. It was a moment familiar to everyone, but most of the time it goes by unnoticed. We can all get a bit self-absorbed.

When the Untouchables finally left the shop, my heart stopped pounding in my chest, my hands stopped trembling, and I could go back to making drinks like I wasn't a caffeine addict. That was such a huge relief, let me tell you. It was like watching the Wicked Witch of the West fly away on her broom with all her flying monkey minions. I was so relieved. So relieved. Not that it changed anything about what happened, but it was just good to know that the minutes that Serena had been torturing me with her fake apology were over.

OIL IN THE WOK

"Hey, are you okay?" I heard Isaac's voice, floating above my head, asking me in the most gentle voice possible. It was so nice to hear his voice. I never thought anyone could make me feel so comforted. It felt like a blanket of tissue paper covering my skin, keeping me safe from the harsh unknowns of the world. Every day I had to constantly fight with the mirror, hoping against hope that I would make it through another day of school, of facing my parents, of facing my friends. Those simple words from Isaac made me forget that for a moment.

I knew a lot of girls who claimed that it was okay for girls to feel totally bad about themselves on certain days when they were feeling low. On those days, tenderly called "self-conscious fat days," a girl is allowed to nitpick everything about herself, from her hair to her clothes, to how fat she looks from behind in a pair of jeans. But it doesn't stop there. I wasn't one to nitpick about my physical attributes, but there were plenty of other things that I obsessed over on those "self-conscious fat days." Usually I nitpicked the embarrassing moments and stuff about my personality that I didn't like. I wondered if that was normal. Was that okay? There was no way to tell, but sometimes I wished I had a simple answer for that.

When someone asks, "Are you okay?" most people reply, "Yeah, I'm okay" or "Yeah, I'm fine," whether they're fine or not. It's reflex. I usually did that too. But that day, I wasn't feeling like brushing off my problems. I wasn't feeling like telling one more lie to one more person. I was not okay and I really wanted to admit it. So I did.

"No, I'm not okay. I'm far from okay. Everything's a mess. Everything is…" As soon as I found my voice, it was amazingly easy to spill everything to Isaac. A few months ago I thought our conversation on marijuana would be the first and last thing we ever talked about, I was so sure that there was no way I'd ever get a chance to become friends with a guy like Isaac. And so sure that we'd never have a decent conversation of any kind. I was so sure because it felt good to be sure of something. But I was wrong.

Isaac was crossing boundaries. I was letting him. Another first. I had never let a boy all the way into my life before and it seemed that although I hadn't let him cross any physical boundaries, I was letting him all the way in.

Isaac responded by smothering me in a hug. I wasn't crying, but a part of me understood that this was the part where he was supposed to comfort the crying, lost, and confused girl, expecting her to comply to him, to hold onto him for dear life, to bury her face into his chest and cover his blue flannel shirt with tears. This was the part where the boy gets to play the Big Protector, the Prince and makes sure all of his girl's problems disappear, where he lets her know that everything was going to be all right and meant it for once.

Did every girl secretly want that, no matter who they were? No matter if the girl was tough inside and had been through every single hardship imaginable to mankind or if she didn't believe in love, platonic or otherwise, didn't every girl want to be hugged like that?

Isaac's hug didn't erase all the pain, didn't get rid of what had happened, couldn't send me back in to time to change something or make the Untouchables change what they did, but it did make me feel better in the moment. And that meant more to me than all the changes that could have been made to fix what happened in the past.

"You're a little flat on the second verse,"

Brooke was saying. It was a week before Christmas and I really wanted to get this demo recorded by then. That would have been the best Christmas present that I gave to myself ever.

I didn't know about singing the way Brooke knew about singing, but I could hear pitch and intonation well. I think that came before these lessons with Brooke, but I never could put it into musical terminology. So I knew she was right about my being flat. That was like my signature. I was always flat in all the wrong places. And never sharp enough in all the right places. She taught me some voice warm-up exercises and I would do them with her, but for some reason, we'd be rehearsing this one part of the song and all of a sudden my voice would pop and it would be too flat. Gosh, sometimes I felt like a ten-year-old boy going through puberty or something! Brooke was being really nice by not laughing every time this would happen. Anyone else and they would have cracked up. I felt like laughing myself most of the time, but I tried not to. Singing was all I had now.

Much to my dismay, Lina and Brooke were still in a fight about Brooke's future. They couldn't drop it and our house was becoming a cacophony of unfinished arguments. Why did discussing one's future always have to end up on a battlefield? It didn't have to be a war between what was right for you and what was right for your family. You didn't have to choose between what other people wanted for you and what you wanted for your future. These things I was sure Lina and Brooke had tucked away in the back of their minds somewhere, but somehow they got lost in the shuffle. I just didn't know how much more fighting this roof could sustain. One day it was going to leak, and when it did, the most negative words were bound to flow down and sink us into the ground.

When everything seemed like it was about

to cave in, what did you do? What could you do? Dad was now complaining to Mom that this house couldn't hold any more angry women. She lashed out at him and the whole cacophonous process started all over again. Such a sickly cycle that I started hiding out at the library whenever it got too intense to study at home.

Lina was just afraid. I knew because even though Mom never said so, she was afraid, too. Wasn't that the case with every teenager's parents? It was the job of parents to raise their children to do good in the world, to be better people, to make a positive contribution to society. They wanted what was best and they had a natural instinct to protect their children from harm and danger. So when it was time to talk about the future, it was never easy. In fact, it was the most terrifying experience ever. Parents and kids each seemed to be fighting for the unknown and the unknown was something absolutely frightening to grapple with.

Mom had finished filling out her side of the divorce papers, but she hadn't signed them yet. I hoped that meant she was having second thoughts. I knew Dad didn't do what she thought he did. The rumors weren't true. They just couldn't be. Meanwhile, I had been looking at some art schools. It seemed that everything I did required a backup plan. I wanted to be a singer, but what if that didn't work out? This was a good time to look at all the forms I had received and start seeing what those schools wanted from me. At the same time, Dad was picking up his own paperwork: forms for getting on *Fashion Forward*, a new show that wasn't a sitcom. *Fashion Forward* featured clothing designers from all over the country who were competing to have the chance to start their own line.

Grand-prize winners would get whatever they needed to start their own avant-garde line and they would get to stay in Fabulous

Las Vegas for a year to do it. My father's dream, besides making sure I was able to follow my own dream, was ultimately to start his own line. He had a bit of a stage fright problem, however, so going on national TV was going to be a big challenge for him. On the other hand, he might not have gotten another chance like this to turn his life around. I just knew that if he could get a spot on *Fashion Forward* then Mom would start believing in him again. Their marriage would be saved! Then there'd be one less unhappy couple in the house...

If only it were that easy.

This week before Christmas was going to be interesting indeed. Whatever happened in the house, I had to finish my demo. At the same time, Mom was going to try to get Dad to fill out his side of the paperwork. Lina was going to continue to shout and try to convince Brooke she was making a big mistake by going to regular school and studying what regular kids studied. Brooke and I were going to have another fight about Isaac, relationships, and what being friends with a guy was supposed to mean anyway. How anyone survived this crazy life was beyond me.

One afternoon I didn't have to work, but Brooke did, so I dropped her off at Co~Z Monster and headed home. Dad was home already when I walked through the door, which happened from time to time, but lately it had been happening more and more. That wasn't a surprise, considering *Fashion Forward* was the most important thing in Dad's life at the moment and he was spending every waking second on it.

I decided I wanted to know the truth. Brooke had mentioned that I was singing like there was something missing, like I didn't know everything I needed to know in order to hit that high B. I was close. I had been hitting B♭ every time. Hey, at least I was precise. She said I needed to find out what I needed to know to make this work or it was just not gonna happen. She didn't know what this piece of info was, but when I thought deep enough about it, I knew what I had to do. And it had been bugging me for some time now...

"Dad," I called. He was muttering to himself as usual, looking over his bust mannequin, working out measurements. He hadn't heard me. That had been happening a lot lately, too.

I decided to go for the subtle approach. When Dad turned to go back to his table, I hid behind the mannequin. Dad looked up, walked over to the bust, and I jumped up and stuck my head over the top, trying to place it where there would have been a head if the bust were real.

"Ah-whoaaa!" He fell backwards, holding a pin and some blue thread in his right hand. "Hey, you scared me there!" Then he started laughing. I had no idea what was going on, but my guess was that he'd been so cooped up in here working on his newest project while dealing with his issues with Mom that he hadn't really had time to have a laugh.

"Did you need something? Your mother should be home soon," my dad said.

"No, I wanted to ask you something actually. We haven't talked in a while. I thought you might want to take a break from your work and talk," I pleaded.

"Sure," he responded. Was this my dad? I was getting so used to him fighting with Mom that his being so calm about everything took me off guard. With this invitation I dove right in.

"What happened?" I asked. "What happened between you and Mom? Is it true that you met someone else?" I found my voice faltering even as I said it. I was unsure now. It was not a state I wanted to be in, but somehow I had found the road here and I couldn't get out.

The truth was I was afraid. I was afraid

that my dad would get angry and wonder why I wanted to know something so personal. I mean, he was my father after all, and even I knew that asking about someone's love life, especially why it went wrong, was no way to approach someone and probably none of my business anyway. Some things were just too personal. But that wasn't it. I wasn't just afraid of that. I was afraid of how he would react to my asking. Would he not answer me and then brush it off as something that kids should not be worrying about? No matter how old I got, he was always going to treat me as his little girl. Dad was my Big Protector for as long as I didn't have a boyfriend to take over that role. For little girls everywhere who looked up to their dad, he was the one to protect them from the harm and evils of the world.

My dad stared at me at first, blank expression on his face. My heart was doing that pounding thing again and once again

I was nervous.

Dad seemed to be considering the ramifications of telling me about his marriage issues. He seemed to be wondering how I got to know so much. Gee, I thought, I only live here every day, watching you and Mom fight incessantly like there's nothing else in the world worse than the two of you together and your problems. You shout so loud I bet the neighbors can hear you from a mile away or more, yet you still pretend like we're one big happy family, like nothing's wrong, like I'm still your little girl and you still have to protect me from *everything*. I just want to know what's going on with you, your life, what you see for your future. I want to know how I can help because besides me who else really knows about your marriage issues? Who else has been there through thick and thin?

There was so much I wanted to say to him, but like always, I didn't. I waited for him to respond. It seemed that I had really stumped him this time.

"My marriage is not something my daughter has to worry about," he said finally. "You're too young. Your job is to study well and get into a good college. Let your mom and me worry about what happened."

The answer he gave me was so cold. Stone cold. The words hung frozen in the air, each one encased in a cube of ice, like a mobile hanging from the ceiling.

Was he right? Was life as somebody's daughter really that simple? It made sense and at the same time made absolutely no sense at all. If I could help him save his marriage, why couldn't I ask him about what happened to tear it apart? So maybe it was none of my business about his love life, but I felt like I had dropped out of the sky and landed in some eleventh dimension where everything was upside down and backwards and I was in a lot of pain with no way out of this mess. I felt trapped. I tried not to interfere or meddle because everyone says that that is bad, but at the same time, I really liked having things resolved. It broke my heart whenever I saw a couple in trouble, even though I had never been a couple with someone.

For someone who had been so generous when it came to helping others with their problems, my dad sure had a hard time accepting help for himself. Sometimes I wondered if this was because men just liked solving problems on their own, with no help from anyone or anything. Or maybe Dad was that way because he'd been doing, earning, gaining all that he had on his own his whole life. It wasn't easy. No one ever said that working towards something that you really wanted was gonna be easy. Still, despite it all, behind his tough exterior, I knew there had to be a way to get through. It couldn't be easy to go through what he had with Mom while trying to relaunch his career. I knew he had been promising for years that he'd make it out there with his own fashion line. But Mom wouldn't stop believing in someone that easily; there had to be something else. Whatever it was, there was a way to fix it, right?

Dad had already started again on his work. Wow. Either he really didn't want to answer my question or it really didn't mean that much to him. But I couldn't just leave. It was absolutely necessary to find out now. I just didn't know how, as obviously the man who went back to his work wanted me to go back to mine.

"Can I help you, Dad?" I asked, unsure of what was to come. I meant, of course, that I could help him with his project. I wasn't even sure if that was allowed in the rules and such, but I wanted to see what I could do.

"No, I've got to finish this on my own. You run along and do your homework. Mom will be home soon." It was the same thing he had said before. This was not a good time to discuss anything with my preoccupied father.

So why couldn't I just leave him alone? Was there a way to get Mom to see that he was still the same old person he was when they first met and were both struggling towards their dreams? If only she would walk in the door right now. I really wanted to continue this conversation, but I knew I would be trekking in dangerous territory if I did, so I let it go, making a mental note to try again another time.

This was getting frustrating, but I still had hope that everything would work itself out in the end.

When I went back to my room to get started on homework, I kept thinking about what Dad was hiding from me. Well, from the family, too. Was it really that bad, that serious? He had never hidden anything quite like this before. It was still bothering me when Mom got home. She started on dinner as usual, but it seemed that her workday hadn't been treating her well because she was grunting while chopping.

OIL IN THE WOK

I was working on a picture that was supposed to represent frustration. Tonight it wasn't going to be hard to find the inspiration for it. First I divided the paper in half vertically. On one side I drew a whole red apple. On the other side I drew one exploding up into countless pieces. Maybe going to art school wouldn't be such a bad idea after all...

Well, as soon as Brooke got home, the idea of art school went straight out of my head. Whenever I saw her I was reminded of my ultimate goal. Some people were like that: you looked at them and you were inspired to do something because they were the hardest-working person you knew, the best singer you knew, the nicest person you knew, the most creative person you knew, the smartest person you knew, man, the list could have gone on forever. When I looked at Brooke, I knew I had to sing.

She had found her way home, sparing me the time to go pick her up, only she got home because Isaac dropped her off. I didn't know why, but as soon as I looked up from my drawing and saw Isaac's car through the window, I felt a pang that ran up and down my heart and through my chest. What did that signify? I knew my brain was telling me that I didn't like him or any guy for that matter, but my heart was telling me something different. Or was I simply jealous that Brooke seemed to have it easier when it came to boys? She seemed to be able to talk to him without any complications of the heart or being nervous or anything. I could be wrong. I mean, a girl could leave all that heart stuff inside, keep it to herself and never reveal it, so it was possible she was just good at keeping it all in. But I figured, even so, I'd still be able to read it on her face.

The face could betray a lot that a mouth never mentions out loud. So far, either Brooke was just a really good actress or her face had nothing to betray. She smiled and waved at Isaac before he drove off. She was just her usual self around him, so why did I suspect there was something more? Why couldn't I just allow our friendship to be one of those Lizzie McGuire friendship triplets? Well, maybe because we weren't in middle school anymore and Isaac was a senior, most likely unavailable after this year, and neither one of us had had a boyfriend in a long time. For me, it was never, and for her, it had been at least six months, maybe a year. I didn't even know much about it.

I honestly didn't think I liked him though. This was a different feeling. I was jealous of something. And it had to do with the ease with which Brooke interacted with Isaac. Plus the fact that Isaac was a cute boy. Was I craving my first relationship, wanting to forget about everything that I had been so steadily working on? To think about love in all its forms for once instead of my dreams, achievements, and goals? Maybe that was it. Maybe that was why I'd been feeling strange lately, like I had to know the answers right away. Of course, a lot of things were still a mystery to me. It was likely not going to get resolved any time soon, but that did not mean I had to give up on everything, right?

The demo is sitting on top of Brooke's suitcase.

Brooke and Lina are packing and I'm staring at my self-portrait for AP Studio Art. I'm handing it in a little bit late, but it's fine— my teacher knows why. I think this is it. It's a girl with her back facing the audience and she's sitting on the beach. She's looking out to the water and there's music notes jumping out over the horizon like dolphins would if they were dolphins instead of music notes. I did a version in colored pencils first before deciding on water colors for the final copy.

This chapter of the Mark and Iris saga is

finally over. They mutually decided it would be best if they separated. Dad signed the papers. I can't say I didn't see this one coming, but a part of me had always hoped they'd be together at least through the release of my first single. Well, here's hoping anyway. Brooke is holding on to my demo for now, and Lina promised she'd help me get it into the hands of Brooke's record producer. Who knows? I just might see my name somewhere else besides the top right hand corner of my AP Bio homework! Mom told Brooke to stay in touch, and that she is welcome any time to drop by to ask Mom questions about medical school.

And now that my self-portrait is done, I'm thinking about calling Celeste. I don't know what I'll say or if there *is* anything that I can say, but I've got to try. Isaac and I decided to remain good friends. I don't know what that's supposed to mean exactly as he is jetting off to college by the end of the summer, but right before graduation he came running to my locker to tell me that he got the walk-on for basketball next year! Then he kissed me on the cheek— something else that also has never happened to me before. I felt my face go red as soon as he did, but then he left me his e-mail address, saying that he wants to keep in touch and let him know how the demo goes. Then we kind of gave each other one last hug and he was off. I don't know if I'll e-mail him, but it was nice of Isaac to do that. All I know is, if I ever get the chance, I definitely want to make it to at least one of his games and see him play.

Dad was shocked when he first found out about my demo and Mom just plain freaked out. But I've given them time to take it all in and process. What with the divorce and having to keep up with Brooke and Lina, the initial shock wore off. Well, for Mom at least. She was impressed—never thought something she helped to create would possess such talent some day. She still wants me to have a backup plan of course, but I'm glad that she's going to let me pursue my dream. It was a different story for my Dad. I think he's freaking out more now that he knows he won't be around, but we both know that isn't true. He's more afraid that I'll end up like him. Well, I'm not him. I hope some day he can see that. For now, I'll just have to settle with him not being around.

I don't know what the future holds for us. I do know that right now, all kinds of love exist under our roof. There is the mother-daughter bond, the father-daughter bond, the best friend-best friend bond, the sister-sister bond, and the husband-wife bond. Well, they aren't all exactly that clear-cut, as love tends to be complicated and as far from simple as possible. But that doesn't matter. Tomorrow is a new day and another chance to work at it, to make it out of the wok and become the dish that we always wanted to be.

In Appreciation:

I want to thank my professors, teachers, and all who lent time and a good eye in helping me realize this novel. I have been immensely inspired by you all and without your wisdom, advice, and encouragement, this story would not have been possible to tell. Special shout out to my wonderful book club ladies, my Tuesday mornings, and of course, my Hut.

YuMin Ye is a freelance writer with a B.A. in Writing Seminars from Johns Hopkins University.

Her short story "Team Bonding" won Honorable Mention in the 2007 *Seventeen* Magazine Fiction Contest, and she received a Finalist Manuscript Award in the 2010 St. Louis Publishers Association competition "Get Ready/Get Published" for *Oil in the Wok.*

She is the St. Louis Book Examiner for Examiner.com. She hopes to change the world one story at a time.